SECRETS
AND SHADOWS

Visit us at www.boldstrokesbooks.com

By the Author

Three Days

One Touch

Secrets and Shadows

SECRETS AND SHADOWS

by

L.T. Marie

2013

SECRETS AND SHADOWS
© 2013 By L.T. Marie. All Rights Reserved.

ISBNe: 9781602829190E
ISBN 13: 978-1-60282-880-3

This Trade Paperback Original Is Published By
Bold Strokes Books, Inc.
P.O. Box 249
Valley Falls, NY 12185

First Edition: June 2013

CREDITS
Editors: Victoria Oldham & Shelley Thrasher
Production Design: Susan Ramundo
Cover Design By Sheri (graphicartist2020@hotmail.com)

Acknowledgments

I wrote *Secrets and Shadows* many years ago. How many years ago, I can't recall. The storyline has gone through at least a half-dozen drafts and another half-dozen edits, but the characters have changed very little. I've written many characters, but Lee and Jo are the closest to my heart. Maybe it's their personalities. Maybe it's their dynamic. Honestly, I have no idea. What I do know is that out of all the stories I've written so far, their story touches me the most, and it is my hope that it strikes a chord within you too.

I have a lot of people I want to thank for helping me along the way. People that have made the story better, stronger.

First off to Lilaine DuSud, one of my first beta readers. You helped me keep the story on track and believable. Without your input, the editing process would have been much more difficult.

To Shelley Thrasher for fine-tuning my story. It runs a lot smoother thanks to your time and expertise.

To my awesome, ever patient, and oh so talented editor, Victoria Oldham. Yeah, I know it's sucking up, but I have to get my brownie points in when I can. Seriously though, this story wouldn't be what it has become without your eye for detail, input, and guidance. Thanks for putting up with me and all my quirks. Anyone who knows me knows that's quite a list.

To Rad, for accepting the story. I don't think I can ever express how much it means to me to be a part of the BSB family. With every book I write, please know one of my goals is to make you proud.

To my wife, Tina. You are the reason I fall asleep at night with a smile on my face and the reason I wake up looking forward to a new day. Thanks for your support and encouragement. I love you.

And finally to you, the readers. Every e-mail, post on Facebook, Tweet, and comment on my blogs telling me how much you enjoy my stories means a lot to me. You All Rock!

Dedication

To my wife Tina,
You are the other half of my heart.
Ti amo

Being deeply loved by someone gives you strength,
while loving someone deeply gives you courage.
Lao Tzu

CHAPTER ONE

People casually strolled along the sidewalk five stories below her with no idea she had chosen today to die.

Lee Winters leaned over the railing of her apartment balcony, her world spiraling out of control. Her perfectly structured world had devolved into chaos, and she had only one logical next step. She lived by the principle that every decision dictated destiny, and as she stood staring over the railing at the pale concrete below, her fate seemed inevitable, inescapable. She'd decided to give up, something her previous persona, retired U. S. Army Staff Sergeant Lee Winters, had never done in her life. Hell, until today, the term "surrender" wouldn't have been a part of her vocabulary.

Clouds dotted the unusually clear February sky. The morning sun was bright and cheery, a direct contrast to the darkness swallowing her soul. She closed her eyes, the warmth of the rays on her face failed to penetrate the cold emptiness inside her. The pain of her barrenness burned like acid, stripping her flesh and reopening old wounds. Today marked the first anniversary of the day her army career had ended—the same day that whatever passion she had for this world and everything in it died, though she hadn't had much to start with. She had no family. Most of her friends were dead. And except for her buddy, Gary, who she saw only occasionally, no one would miss her. She was alone, she was tired of fighting. The nightmare had to end.

Jumping would be the coward's way out. Suicide went against everything she'd once believed in. At one time she'd been anything but a coward. Some even called her a hero. But those memories were mere shadows of her past. She would've sold her soul to have died sacrificing herself for someone else, someone she cared about, instead of standing on a balcony contemplating the sidewalk far below.

The morning had started like every other day since she returned from the war. Her muscles ached, her body stiff and vulnerable. Shucking off her blankets during sleep, she'd awakened to the early morning chill, her sheets soaked with sweat from her nightly terror. Her thick dark hair stuck to her forehead and neck, the down feathers of her pillow crushed in her fist. She'd been violent during sleep only after being discharged. One morning she'd woken up with her fist embedded in the wall, her knuckles and skin broken and bleeding. These irrational behaviors were just one of the many reasons she avoided people—why she eluded intimacy at all costs and why she'd never be able to share her life with someone, knowing she could unintentionally injure them.

Gripping the railing tight, she grunted. "Fuck." A sharp pain made her sag against the thick wrought iron. Every shallow breath equaled inhaling fire as she waited for the burning sensation that bolted like lightning down her left arm to lessen. The pain constantly reminded her of everything she'd lost in the past year.

Death should have welcomed her in Ramadi a year ago, but no. Fate had dealt her a tormented existence that made her relive daily the horror of what war could do to a person's psyche. If that wasn't bad enough, her nightmares were worse than the flashbacks. PTSD, the professionals called it. She called it hell for the living.

"Post Traumatic Stress Disorder affects thousands of people," the shrink had told her when she first returned from the war-ravaged land and tried to settle into civilian life. Trouble sleeping and eating were the first on a long list of symptoms. Irritability and feeling inadequate around people caused her to shut herself away from the world. Concentrating on a single thought for more than a few minutes at a time had become nearly impossible. This, above all else, concerned her, considering that in the service she'd had to handle multiple stressful situations at once and answer every question quickly and decisively. When they'd handed her the discharge papers, she left the only life she'd ever known. In the field, most of her decisions concerned life and death. Now, she sat around most days staring mindlessly at the television or checking CNN updates on the war's progress. But when focusing on the tiniest of details became an exercise in masochism, she finally stopped trying to be like everyone else and shut herself away.

A five-story drop should end all the pain—her last decision. She was straddling the railing, similar to the way she straddled her motorcycle, when the telephone rang, shattering the silence of the early morning. She hesitated, one booted foot still on the balcony.

Just a bit farther.

It kept ringing.

The leg taking her weight began to shake as she stared at the phone. What the hell. She could wait a few more minutes. Besides, no one had called her in months, and she couldn't help wondering who it could be, now, of all times. She swung her leg back over the railing and swore at the pain. She glanced at the street below when she grabbed the phone, swallowing the lump in her throat.

"Winters."

"Well, good *fucking* morning to you too, sunshine," Gary said. "I see someone's cranky this morning. What's the matter? Sleeping past seven becoming a habit now that you're a civilian?"

"I've been up since 0500." Nothing had changed in the last ten years. "What do you want? I'm busy."

Gary Franks seemed to be the only person who really understood Lee and was more like a pesky brother than a man who'd served two years under her command. He'd lost one of his legs after shielding another soldier from a bomb that leveled a building in Iraq. He was wheelchair bound because he still refused the use of a prosthetic, but somehow even with his physical disability he had come back in better mental and physical shape than she had.

"Bullshit! Busy doing what?" Gary said. "You haven't done shit since you've been back except try a couple of small, meaningless jobs. But I got something for you, buddy, that's going to change all that. Something long term."

Lee had given up on the idea of a job after the last one ended badly. She hadn't meant to break the asshole's arm, but she'd warned him before he got in her face. Since then, she'd been considered a ticking time bomb, far too dangerous to hire. Given the fact that a few moments ago she'd almost become another piece of chewing gum stuck to the pavement, maybe they were right. Besides, who was going to hire her? She had only one good arm. Physically she was in the worst shape of her life, not to mention she had alienated everyone since being discharged from the army hospital. No one liked her. Hell, she didn't like herself.

"Hey, you still there?" Gary asked.

"Yeah…I'm listening. Talk to me about this job," she said, a little harsher than she intended.

"Well," he drawled out in one long syllable. "Have you ever heard of the group Total Femme?"

"What the hell kind of name is that? Sounds like one of those cheap perfumes people can buy at the local thrift shop."

"I take it that's a no."

"Jesus, get on with it, will you?"

"You're unbelievable. How could you not know who these women are, Lee? They're the hottest female pop group in the country. Their faces are plastered on every magazine cover and newspaper from California to New York. You'd have to be locked in your apartment twenty-four seven not to know anything about them."

"Yeah…so?" Gary never could get to the point.

"Come on, Sarge. You can't tell me you've never heard of them?"

The familiar title made her stiffen. No one had called her that since the day she received her discharge papers. That identity didn't apply to her anymore. "Gary."

"Well...uh...anyway. I just got a call from Marilyn Stockard, their new manager. They need a personal female bodyguard for the lead singer's sister. They're willing to pay big bucks and I thought of you. What do you say?"

I say you're fucking insane if you think I need a babysitting job! This had to be a joke. How the hell was she going to protect someone else when she could barely lift her left arm or think beyond the moment? No way would she let him rope her into this. She was out of shape. She was as unstable as a stick of dynamite in the desert heat. Besides, she had plans today. "No, thanks. I'll pass."

"Excuse me," Gary said. "Pass? Are you *crazy?*"

"Certifiable," Lee said, and laughed, wincing internally at the bitterness in her tone. If he only knew the half of it.

"Lee, you're not listening to me. This is *big* money. They specifically asked for a woman. Ten thousand up front, plus a thousand a day. You can't pass this up. *Hell,* if I could walk, I'd throw on a fucking dress and do it myself."

"How much did you say?"

"You heard me."

"You know, I still think I'll pass. I don't need money that bad." *Especially since I can't take it where I'm going.*

"Sure you do. But more important, you need this job. Tell me you're not jumping at a chance to put some of your skills to work?"

Interesting choice of words. But unfortunately he was right. She'd felt so useless for so long. What the hell. She could spare a few hours. It wasn't like she had a deadline. "Tell you what. I'll hear what you have to say, but I'm not making any promises."

"Great! Let's meet for logistics in about an hour? You know I don't like to discuss personal stuff over the phone."

Lee was well aware of Gary's cautious nature. He didn't trust anyone except her and maybe a handful of other people he'd served with in the five years he spent in the military. In the army his buddies nicknamed him The Yellow Pages, a title he deserved for his intelligence-gathering capabilities. She never questioned how he got his information. Some things were better left kept secret.

"Location?" Lee asked, grabbing her keys and jacket.

"Coffee and donuts," Gary said, which translated to the Rolling Pin on 4th. "0900, and Lee?"

"What?"

"Look cute."

"Bite me."

Lee stepped out of the Victorian apartment complex, thinking for the second time in her life how life could change in an instant. She mounted her bike, the powerful machine roared to life between her thighs, and she looked up at the railing she'd been halfway over ten minutes earlier. For the first time in what felt like forever, maybe the world had tilted in her favor.

❖

Lee parked her Yamaha FZR1000 close to the curb and took off her blue-and-white helmet. After unzipping her heavy motorcycle jacket she found a seat on the patio of the popular outdoor café. She glanced at her special-ops watch, noting the time. Gary would appear in three, two, one…

"Hey, buddy," Gary said, bumping her chair with his wheelchair from behind.

Lee moved so Gary could maneuver safely to the other side of the table, not offering help out of respect for his independence. Pride was important for a soldier, and seeing her only friend confined to a wheelchair was still sometimes hard to digest. God only knew what it did to him mentally.

His two-wheeled device was a constant reminder of how war changed people. True, she had her own personal demons to deal with, but watching someone else suffer was always harder on Lee than suffering herself.

"Hey, Lee," Gary said. "You look zoned. Did you even hear what I just said?"

For the second time that day, she found her mind wandering. She'd heard him but she hadn't really been listening. For a second, she'd even forgotten where she was and why she'd agreed to meet him. These lapses in focus happened constantly, but she'd never admit that to Gary or anyone else. "Just dandy. Now that we got the formalities out of the way, why don't you tell me everything I need to know?"

Lee's no-nonsense attitude was probably one of the many reasons Gary had chosen her for the job at hand. She sat across from him, legs crossed at the ankles, not a wrinkle in her jeans or T-shirt. She might have lost a little weight and become even more emotionally detached than she'd always been, but she still presented herself as someone who paid meticulous attention to detail. The only thing drastically different about her was that her hair currently fell slightly below her collar in a shaggy sort of way instead of high and tight, like she'd worn it when she served. She also still possessed the ability to look at someone without her expression giving anything away, a skill that had come in handy more times than she could count. This was one of them.

Lee folded her arms over her chest, not particularly happy with the way Gary was staring inquisitively at her. When she asked someone a question in the service, they answered without hesitation. His scrutiny irritated her but she kept her restlessness channeled. She would appear to him as she always appeared to others—unbreakable, void of any emotion. Nothing could penetrate the barriers that had made her the soldier she used to be or the civilian she was pretending to be.

"Well." Gary nervously cleared his throat. "Since you don't know much about Total Femme, let me enlighten you. They're a group of five women who made it big about two years ago. They can't go anywhere without a mob scene. Reporters, paparazzi, and crazed fans follow them everywhere. Each band member has a minimum of three bodyguards who travel with her at all times. Security has been a nightmare and it's only going to get worse."

Gary handed Lee a picture of five stunning women. Each leather-clad member sported knee-high spiked boots and see-through mesh tops. One particular woman stood out among the rest because of her flawless beauty. She was the tallest of the five, with shoulder-length brown hair that surrounded the coolest, bluest eyes she'd ever seen. The contrast of light and dark only made the woman more stunning, but this woman's looks were apparently as phony as her costume.

"Stop dickin' around," she said with annoyance. The photo told her nothing except that every straight man and lesbian in the country most likely had a framed copy of this exact picture on their nightstand. Hell, she couldn't blame them. "What else you got?"

"So impatient." Gary chuckled, the tension easing from his body as he handed her another photo.

The second picture wasn't airbrushed. The woman in the current photo closely resembled the taller woman in the first one, but with sweeping distinctions.

She sat on a blanket with her legs curled underneath her, smiling up at the camera, her hair the color of wheat blowing in the summer breeze and a smile so genuine Lee felt the innocence touch her through the photo. The woman's eyes were a cool Caribbean blue, but Lee picked up a hint of sadness in them immediately. "Who is she?"

"*This* is Jolene West. Tory West is the lead singer," he said, pointing to the hottest woman in the first picture, "and Jolene is her identical twin and your job assignment. Unlike Tory, Jolene doesn't sing but has always traveled with the group as Tory's manager. At times in the past Tory also used her sister as a body double, but since Jolene's accident, she hasn't been able to do anything in any capacity."

"Twin sister?" They looked nothing alike.

"Identical."

"Then—"

Gary put up his hand. "Tory wears a wig and contacts when she performs."

Ah. "And what about this accident?"

"It's all there in the file. I've compiled—"

"Jesus, Gary, just tell me, damn it." Lee was growing uneasy, an unfamiliar feeling in general, and not being able to instantly tell why pissed her off.

"The sisters have been fighting for years about various issues, but lately most of the fights centered around Tory not appreciating Jolene as a manager. Tory's a control freak and has always questioned Jolene's ability, even though she insists she doesn't want anyone else as a manager. One night, Tory asked Jolene to fill in for her at a fund-raising event to raise money for childhood diabetes. Jolene agreed but told Tory that when she returned home, she would be resigning as her manager and moving out of the house they share. Jolene never made it home that night because someone intentionally rammed into her limo and put her in the hospital."

For the first time in a while, Lee's attention didn't falter. She hated it when people got hurt, and it bothered her that the innocent-looking woman in the picture had become a victim. Movie stars and big-profile individuals always irritated her when they disregarded their own personal safety and ignorantly questioned authority. Her last job had proved that. The supposed former drug dealer gone rap star thought he was above the law. When he wanted Lee to stand by while he tried to coax some young girl into doing cocaine with him, which she clearly didn't look interested in, Lee intervened. He'd told her to mind her own fucking business, and when she didn't back down, he took a swing at her. He was lucky she'd only broken his arm and not strangled him with the five-pound gold cross he wore around his neck. "Did they catch the person who did it?"

"No. And there's more to the story." Gary reached into another folder and handed Lee a postmarked letter in a plain envelope.

She read the note twice, committing the words to memory. Tory West clearly had a stalker and words such as "I'm watching you" and "You're mine" clued her in to the serious nature of the person's obsession. The letter was written using letters or words cut out from printed pages. "When did she receive this?"

"A few weeks ago, and it's only one of many from the same psycho."

"And how long has she been receiving them?"

"A few months. They started out like the letter in your hand. 'I love you. I want you,' that sort of crap. She didn't think anything of it at first, but then they became aggressive, threatening. She used to get one every week. Now she gets three or four a week. This is one of the earlier letters."

"So why didn't she do something sooner?"

"You know how it is." Gary shrugged. "Celebrities receive letters from people all the time. Most is fan mail, but unfortunately every once in a while it's some obsessed kook. She didn't take it seriously until this maniac attacked Jolene and wrote her another letter claiming it was him."

"Him? So the attacker's definitely male?"

"Good question. We think so. Well, the profiler does anyway. Statistically speaking, eighty-seven percent of stalkers are men, so unless something suggests this wacko is a woman, we're going with the guy probability."

Profiler. Good. That meant Gary already had someone working on the inside.

He had a network of friends, most either current or former FBI employees. She never cared where he got his information nor did she want to know. All that mattered was that it was accurate. "And where's the letter that stated he did it?"

"It's being analyzed by another *friend* of mine. Even though this whack job cuts out letters and doesn't write them, we were hoping for some type of DNA from saliva or something, but so far, nothing. In fact, every letter he's ever written is clean. Believe me, I checked. I can have it for you by tonight, though, if you want to see it."

"Do you have any other leads?"

Gary ran his hands through his sandy-colored hair. "No. Whoever hit her left the scene and the police haven't found any incriminating evidence. Another friend of mine's doing some tests on the sly, but I haven't heard back from him yet."

Lee considered the information for a moment, but something was nagging at her. "So why go after Jolene West? Why not Tory West, if that's who he's obsessed with?"

"According to the last letter that I'm going to get for you, she was an example. At first we thought he'd made a mistake since Tory was supposed to be at that event, not Jo pretending to be her, but it turns out he'd targeted Jo on purpose. He says he'll take away everything Tory cares about until she realizes her love for him. Tory and the other band members have guards already, and the girls don't have any other family left. Jolene is the only one without a bodyguard, which is why he went after her, obviously."

"Does she know?"

"Yes. And she's pissed."

I bet. "So she needs protection and that's why I'm here."

"Yes, but…" Gary began to fidget. Something was definitely up. "She needs the protection because Tory is worried he really will go after Jolene again, but she's refusing help."

"Then what the hell am I supposed to do?"

"Convince her."

Oh, hell no! "This is bullshit. First you want me to babysit, and now you want me to get in the middle of their family squabbles? Forget it."

"Shit," he mumbled as Lee got up and stepped onto the sidewalk. "Lee, wait!"

She stopped and turned. A few patrons had jumped and stared at him with shocked expressions, but no one was more surprised than Lee. Gary wouldn't draw attention to himself unless the situation was serious. Glancing down to where his leg should have been, she remembered the last time he'd drawn fire. He'd saved one of his good friends but lost a limb for his bravery.

When he had stood tall, Gary's six feet, four inches made him
an intimidating presence. With his rugged good looks and piercing
blue eyes, he'd always been labeled a ladies' man. He was still
handsome, but in that chair with the light gone from his eyes, she
could tell he'd also returned home a shadow of who he used to be.
She returned to her seat, nodding for him to continue. His sweaty
brow and nervous fidgeting indicated that, after drawing attention
to himself, he wanted to do anything but.

"Maybe we should, uh…"

"Take a walk."

"Yeah." Gary smiled gratefully. "But how about you walk and
push?"

They maneuvered safely through the crowded patio and
headed toward Gary's car. The second they were alone his anxiety
quieted. "The situation is complicated, Lee."

Like she hadn't heard that before. Of course it was complicated.
Why else would they pay that kind of money for protection and
have someone like Gary search out someone like her?

"Even though he's claiming it was him, we have no way to
know it's the truth," he said. "This guy is smart, and if Jolene
doesn't take the protection seriously this could turn out bad.
Tory's worried that whoever it is won't just injure Jo the next
time. It's obvious this maniac could have killed her and, according
to my sources, he'll escalate the violence. That's apparent in the
frequency of his letter writing. Supposedly, he was only trying to
prove a point. For now. Besides being intelligent he's resourceful.
Jolene is aware that she was the intended target, but she's stubborn
and, well, proud."

"I don't care about any of that. How am I supposed to protect
someone who doesn't want protecting?"

"Jolene doesn't want it because she always tries to prove to
everyone she's not Tory. She's lived in Tory's shadow most of her
life, and once Tory became famous, it only got worse. In her mind,
accepting a bodyguard makes her look like her sister, yet again."

Lee sighed, shaking her head. This was the kind of shit that made her miss the military. In the service things were cut and dried. You were either told what to do or you ordered someone to do it—period—no questions asked. You never had to explain your actions to anyone. People's feelings were never an issue. "You know, I don't really give a fuck about this domestic crap. Besides, I'm still not understanding how you're going to get Jolene West to accept my help if she doesn't want it."

"Tory talked with Jolene about having a bodyguard yesterday. She's agreed to work with a female shadow, but only in limited capacities until she's healed. Since all Tory's bodyguards are male and Jolene doesn't want a male shadow, I suggested you. Oh, and by the way, she likes the word *shadow* because *bodyguard* makes her feel claustrophobic."

Lee continued to process the information but still couldn't account for a piece of the puzzle. She wouldn't accept the job until she knew every detail. "What else?"

"There is one more thing. Jolene West has certain *tastes*."

She stared at him, not following. "You've got ten seconds or I'm walking."

"She's…Oh, hell. She's gay."

"So? When has that ever mattered…" Lee hesitated. Suddenly the picture became clearer. "Wait a second. Is that why I'm getting this job?"

"That's part of it." He shrugged. "In my experience, men seem to have more of a problem with this kind of thing than someone with your background."

"My *background*?" If Gary hadn't been confined to a wheelchair Lee would probably have hit him. Yes, she preferred women, but her limited experience in the past didn't make her an expert.

"Be reasonable," he said. "If she does want to date or go out eventually, she'll want privacy, and no one blends into different environments better than you. I mean, look at you." He pointed at her, making her look down at her clothes. "Shaggy hair, jeans and boots. You don't look anything like a bodyguard. You can successfully blend into civilian life, which is one reason I picked you for the job. Not that I need to tell you this, but frankly you're the best. And Tory wants the best for her sister."

She had made a great squad leader partially because she could teach the younger recruits the art of blending into all types of surroundings. If she didn't want to be seen, then she wouldn't be. She truly was the best of the best—a person who would cast no shadow, able to live in the dark until she chose to reveal herself. It was also why she'd been the only woman ever accepted into the elite Rangers' program, only to have lost that opportunity the day she was injured. Rangers were known for their skill at remaining undetected in a war. In a combat situation if you saw a Ranger, it was probably too late. She sighed. Gary's reasons for picking her were valid, but they still rankled her. Jolene West didn't mind having a shadow as long as she kept to the shadows. But to protect Jolene West, Lee would have to be within a certain range at all times.

"As I said before, this is bullshit. You think you can throw out a few compliments and I'll cave? You can forget it. Since when has my personal life ever had any bearing on my work?"

"Damn it, Lee!" Gary said, his composure gone. "She's in serious trouble and we don't know any woman with your type of experience that can help. Please."

Please? Gary didn't beg. First calling attention to himself and now begging? Another piece of the puzzle was still missing. "What else?"

"That's it. You have everything," he said, avoiding eye contact with her for the first time.

She didn't work this way. No information—no job. That's how it had always been, and she wasn't about to bend her rules just because money was involved. "No, I don't. See ya around." She turned but was quickly stopped. She glanced at his trembling hand on her arm before meeting his barren eyes and whispered, "What else?"

Gary bowed his head, speaking just above a hoarse whisper. "Tory and I were…engaged…to be married. It was before I was shipped off to Iraq. When I returned, my leg was gone and so was Tory. I couldn't let her live with only parts of me left, and I don't just mean the physical parts. Mentally, I've changed too. You know."

Engaged? Her mind reeled with the new information. She thought back to when they served. They'd hung out numerous times after a mission and she seemed to recall Gary bragging about a woman, but why couldn't she remember the conversations? Could the PTSD be blocking some of these memories? The doctors said that could happen. But maybe she'd been so focused on her missions she hadn't cared to hear about other people's personal lives. When she'd had something to carry out, nothing could distract her. Ever. But here was one time when she wished she'd paid more attention to Gary's constant ramblings. It pained her as she watched the once-proud boulder of a man sitting before her shrink to the size of a pebble. Even though she was surprised by his admission, she couldn't offer him comfort by divulging her own pain. Some things were better left buried.

"We tried working things out when I returned, but between my disabilities and her career, we decided it was best to stop seeing each other. When she contacted me about the stalker, she knew I could help. I told her about friends, like you, who can deal with all types of situations *off* the radar. She doesn't want to involve the authorities and draw attention to herself, and she's asked me to do this favor. I can't let her down. Not again."

Lee stared into the distance, the sounds of everything around her fading like the late morning sun behind the clouds. She'd only ever had one weakness, and that was helping a fellow soldier in need. She couldn't say no to him and live with herself. "Okay, I'll do it, but I have some stipulations."

"Name it."

"First, I don't take orders from anyone. That includes Tory West, her bodyguards, or God himself. I may be accepting a job as a bodyguard, but I'm no grunt. If I see something I don't like and want it changed, it gets done. Period. No questions asked. If anyone undermines my authority or decisions, I walk. Do I make myself clear?"

"Crystal," he said, smiling. Obviously he expected nothing less from her.

"Good. When do I start?"

"Tomorrow, 0700," he said, a spark back in his eyes. "And, Lee—thanks."

Lee retrieved the folder from him and tucked it under her arm. "Don't thank me yet. She hasn't met me. And from the sound of it, I probably won't last a day."

CHAPTER TWO

Jo opened her eyes cautiously, afraid that the Richter-scale-sized headache she'd suffered in the past week would still rock her fragile state. Her concussion had been worse than the doctors anticipated, but as each day passed the fogginess had begun to abate, leaving behind pounding pain. Grimacing as she shifted onto her side, she was reminded of the cracked ribs that would take weeks to heal.

"Ow, damn." She moaned and collapsed back onto the bed. Getting into a comfortable position was impossible due to the fluorescent-pink fiberglass cast that extended from her foot to just below her knee. The doctors had explained that her ankle had shattered in three places—the extensive surgery had required plates and screws to keep the bones firmly in place. The healing time was unknown due to the nature of the injury, but she would have a cast for at least eight weeks, with a full round of physical therapy to follow.

She hated feeling helpless, and between the cracked ribs, broken ankle, and raging headache it was hard to feel anything but. Added to all the other symptoms, nausea made her want to remain inert most of the time, a side effect of the concussion. Bright lights only intensified the nausea. Photo something or other, the doctors called it. Whatever, the name didn't matter as long as it went away.

She fought reaching for the pain medication again, even though she desperately wanted another pill. After the first few days she'd tried to wean herself off the drugs unless the pain reduced her to tears. The meds left her groggy and constipated, but the doctors told her not to be a hero and to take the prescription if needed.

Pushing slowly out of bed, she adjusted the crutches underneath her arms, the change in altitude sending a quick surge of blood down to her injured limb. Immediately she began to have second thoughts regarding the "tough it out" mentality, but instead of reaching for the pill bottle, she gingerly made her way to the bathroom until she was able to balance against the sink.

The cold water was a poor substitute for the cup of coffee that was her normal breakfast staple, but her long-time family physician had warned her away from caffeine, saying it could prolong the side effects of the medication. The tongue-lashing she gave him made him laugh but prompted him to give her one of his stern talks, with the promise that she'd be able to indulge in her obsession once the headaches and nausea subsided.

"Well, he didn't say I couldn't. He just emphasized I shouldn't," she mumbled right before another wave of nausea hit. White-knuckling the sink, she pitched forward as her stomach rebelled, producing another round of dry heaves. Maybe skipping dinner last night hadn't been one of her better decisions, since taking pain medication on an empty stomach wasn't advisable.

Tracing the fading bruise above her left eye and the multiple cuts surrounding her right one, she grunted in disgust. The discoloration and scarring would take weeks to heal and probably require plastic surgery. What made the injuries worse was Tory's overreaction when Jo had woken up inside the hospital. At first, she couldn't decide what had upset Tory more, the injuries to her face or the fact that she'd been injured in Tory's place. Whatever her motivation, it was because of Tory's career that she had become a victim of her sister's life. Again.

Jo was tired. Tired of being Tory West's sister, tired of living in Tory's shadow, but most of all, tired of the things she couldn't change. Being a twin had always made her feel special. There'd been a time when all she'd had to do was look at Tory and feel the connection that only two people with the same DNA could share. That connection had offered her comfort for most of her life, made her feel safe, loved. But over the last few years, she had experienced a strange detachment, an indifference that angered her and made it impossible to reason with her sister.

Tory's career hadn't started the rift in their relationship, but it certainly hadn't helped repair the gap that had slowly developed from the time they were teenagers. After suffering the loss of both their parents, they'd managed to stick by each other while Tory struggled early on in her career. Jo had even accepted Tory's offer to be her manager and publicity double when the group's popularity skyrocketed, in hopes that the time together could help them work out some of their differences.

At first, Jo's fresh ideas along with Total Femme's unique chemistry proved to be an award-winning combination. She'd traveled everywhere with Tory—filled in for her when needed— put her life on hold, leaving little time to develop relationships outside of her sister's career. This time, though, she vowed to put her own needs first. As she lay in bed with nothing to do but think, she wondered when she'd forgotten about her own life. When had her life become completely overshadowed by Tory's?

Their last argument had been the night of the accident, and the disagreement was always the same. Tory took her superstar role for granted and believed she could do whatever she wanted, whenever she wanted. No matter how hard Jo tried to keep Tory on schedule, Tory was always late for guest appearances or would book something without telling her, which meant Jo would have to fill in for her elsewhere. When the last push-pull ended in a stalemate, she had screamed a few harsh words and told Tory she'd resign as her manager the next day.

Besides their tenuous working relationship, Tory also couldn't seem to understand that Jo wanted her own life—she couldn't get past her own money and fame to recognize Jo's needs. But what made Jo the angriest she'd ever been was waking up in the hospital to discover Tory had already replaced her with popular celebrity manager Marilyn Stockard.

Yes, Jo wanted out. But it should have been her decision. Once again, Tory had made a choice for her without so much as a discussion. She'd told Jo that she appreciated everything she'd done for her career and knew that Jo's knack for contract negotiations, dealing with publicists, and taking on the tour promoters had been a great asset to her at the beginning. She'd also said that she was tired of the fighting and thought this was for the best. Even through the medication and the pain, Jo was lucid enough to see past Tory's bullshit excuse and comprehend that all she'd ever really been was a tool. That realization hurt in a way she hadn't expected.

But blaming it all on Tory wouldn't be fair. She'd agreed to help her sister further her career with the promise from Tory that their relationship would never suffer because of it. All she'd ever wanted was to be connected to her twin and go back to the way things were before their parents died, before Tory had become famous. But it was too late. Not only could they not go back, but the last thing to keep her connected to Tory—her looks—were shattered like the car windows that had exploded upon impact, scarring Jo's face to the point that she and Tory were no longer identical, no matter how much makeup they used.

Tory had fussed over Jo's care ever since, evidently trying to mend fences and making sure she received the royal treatment. But Jo didn't want Tory's guilt and pity. All she wanted was her sister's love, but after everything that happened, they had nothing more between them except genetics.

The rapping of knuckles on wood startled her. She wasn't in the mood for company and was about to tell whoever it was to go away when Tory pushed into the room.

"Jo, you know you're not supposed to be out of bed," Tory said. She guided Jo back to the bed, pulling back the covers for her, and sat next to Jo once she was settled. "How are you feeling?"

"Better than yesterday," Jo said wearily.

"Are you sure? You know I can get Doctor Chase over here if you—"

"Cut the shit, Tory. What do you want?" Jo's words were harsh, but she wasn't in the mood for the pity party. Besides, Tory's refusal to look her in the eye meant she wasn't there just to check on her. She'd done something Jo wouldn't like.

"How do you know I want something?" Tory said, smoothing out a nonexistent wrinkle on the blanket.

"You're kidding me, right?" Jo laughed even though her ribs didn't approve. "You're my twin, for Christ's sake! I can tell when you have to go to the bathroom before you do."

"My, aren't we feisty this morning."

"Every morning." *If you ever paid attention to me maybe you'd notice.* "By the way, you suck at changing the subject. Tell me why you're here."

"Well, since you asked so nicely, I've hired a new bodyguard for you. She arrives first thing tomorrow."

"What!" Jo vaulted to a sitting position, the motion sending a shooting pain through her belly and leg. "Ow…damn. I told you, no fucking bodyguard."

"Jesus, Jo," Tory said, placing her arms on Jo's shoulders. "Stop moving before you hurt yourself more."

"Let me go!" Jo batted her hands away.

"You're so stubborn! Why won't you let me help you?"

"Don't you think you've *helped* enough?" Jo said in a deadly tone. Venom would be dripping from her fangs if she'd had them. How dare Tory go against her wishes? "I don't want a new bodyguard, and I definitely didn't want that stick-in-the-mud you had following me around the house the other day. So whoever is coming over here tomorrow can go to hell, and you can join her!"

"I'm sorry you feel that way," Tory said. "But what's done is done. I only want you safe, even if you're too stubborn to realize it."

"I told you—"

"Yes, I heard you the first time. But you didn't say no to *having* a bodyguard. You just said it had to be a woman. A shadow, remember? Since the attack, the girls and I are expanding our protection as well. Come on, what's the big deal? When you used to go out pretending to be me, you had three or four at a time. One won't put a kink in your plans."

"Plans...humph." *Like that'll happen anytime soon.* "I look like fucking Frankenstein. I want a woman to run to me, not away from me. And I sure as hell don't have any plans. So a bodyguard isn't necessary, since I can't even leave the house."

Tory laughed. "That's the Jo I know."

She wanted to tell Tory she didn't know shit, but her headache was bordering on brain-tumor status and her eyes felt like they might explode from their sockets. "What time is she coming?"

"In the morning. Please, Jo," Tory said, linking fingers with her. "You can't blame me for wanting this. How can you possibly expect me to leave you unprotected after the accident, especially while you're injured? What if this psycho who hit you broke in here and hurt you again? If something happened to you..."

The sound of anguish in Tory's voice surprised Jo. Tory had never been an emotional person and most of the time was as coolly isolated as a chunk of iceberg floating in a remote sea. Usually this behavior pissed Jo off, but she could always deal with Tory's selfishness because she'd been doing it all her life. However, this new caring and sensitive side left Jo at a loss for words. Instinctively, she squeezed Tory's hand.

"Sis, I'm sorry for yelling at you but don't you see? Even though this guy came after me, it was only a one-time thing. Those letters are about you, not me. All I am is a statement."

"Don't say that—"

"Stop! I don't want to hear how we can't prove it was him. I know in my heart it was this guy, and you know it too. The only people who don't know it are the authorities and your fans, because you refuse to acknowledge you have a problem. I understand you don't want your fans to find out it wasn't you in the limo that night, and I agree that bringing the authorities in will disrupt our lives. Honestly, though, after reading the rags, I can't believe *they* haven't figured it out yet or started running conspiracy theories."

"You're not the only one," Tory mumbled.

"So you see, I'm glad you're being protected. I truly am. But why can't you understand I don't want this life anymore and that I never wanted to be under the constant scrutiny of you and these watchdogs? In a few months, when I'm healed, I'm gonna get out of here and do something with my life."

"I do understand," Tory said sadly. "But for those few months, can you at least accept the protection? Please. It would really make me feel better."

Of course it would. But do you even care about what it's likely going to do to me? Jo sighed and closed her eyes, exhausted. "Whatever. But if I don't like her, I have the right to pick someone else. You're done making decisions for me. Got it?"

"Understood." Tory kissed Jo's forehead. "Now try and get some rest."

"Wait!" Jo grabbed Tory's hand. "Who is she?"

"Someone who comes highly recommended. Sleep now. We'll talk more tomorrow."

"Fine. But I want to see her resume *before* I meet her."

"Resume?"

"Yes...resume." Jo rolled her eyes in exasperation. Did Tory really think she'd allow her to hire someone she knew nothing about?

"I didn't think to ask for one."

There's a big surprise. "It's probably called a jacket, docket, portfolio, or whatever those military goons you use regularly call it, where I get to see details regarding this woman's life and her qualifications."

Tory raised an eyebrow. "How did you know she's military?"

"Duh! Tell me Gary had nothing to do with this?"

"I wouldn't even try." Tory smiled. "Can I get you something while I'm out?"

Yeah, a one-way ticket out of here. "No…nothing. Thanks."

"I'll be home in a few hours. I love you." Tory closed the door and the house was silent once again.

Shutting her eyes, Jo inhaled deeply in an attempt to regain her equilibrium. She had no idea who this new bodyguard was, but if she had anything to say about it, the woman wouldn't last a week.

Chapter Three

S urgical gloves? Why would you need those, you pathetic idiot?" the Angry Man asked with a sneer.

"I don't know," the man screamed. "I don't remember."

It had taken him hours to cut out letters from dozens of periodicals. He quickly assembled them until his message was clear. Fingerprints weren't a worry. He laughed at his brilliance while his tormentor, whom he always only thought of as the Angry Man, berated him for his stupidity.

"It's perfect," he whispered as he dabbed the adhesive of the white standard-sized envelope with a sponge before carefully sealing his thoughts inside.

"You fool! These letters are a waste of time. She doesn't love you. She doesn't even know you."

"Shut up! You're the fool. Of course she knows who I am. I've written her dozens of letters. She knows *all* my thoughts."

"Not all of them."

He turned away, not willing to face his tormentor any longer. "You're right. Not all of them."

"So what are you going to do if this pathetic little plan of yours doesn't work?"

"It *will* work."

"That's what you said every other time, and look where you are now."

"Shut up!" This time he held a paperweight firmly in his hand.
"Go ahead. Throw it."

He lowered the weight and winced at the look of sadistic triumph in his tormentor's black eyes.

"Like I said before, *pathetic*."

He ignored the Angry Man, returning to the task at hand. Tory *would* take him seriously. Otherwise she would pay for disregarding his love for her.

He stared at the picture he'd stolen years ago, remembering the first time he'd seen her, on the arm of another man who hadn't been worthy. She was the love of his life. Now, every inch of space in his tiny room was covered with pictures of her. Everywhere he looked, he felt her staring into his soul.

His tormentor repeatedly yelled at him, but he ignored the taunts by humming one of his favorite tunes. He smiled as he affixed the stamp. This time she wouldn't turn him down. This time she would obey his demands or she'd regret it.

CHAPTER FOUR

L ee stood on the front porch of the West home patiently waiting for someone to answer the door. She used the time to study the expansive grounds, soaking in every detail of the picturesque estate, from the professionally manicured front yard to the property above and beyond the large home. No surveillance equipment was visible. All the windows on the bottom level of the home were open, the curtains billowing in the morning breeze. The house was completely exposed, which meant that Jolene West was completely exposed. As soon as her meeting with Tory West ended, she would talk to Gary and explain how unhappy she was with whoever was in charge of the piss-poor security details.

The West Estate exemplified the definition of ostentatious. Nestled in the hills of Portola Valley, the twelve-bedroom colonial-style home with its giant stone pillars and large bay windows covered a generous section of the grounds and overlooked a large gorge. The only way onto the property was by entering a security code at the front gate, which Lee knew was useless and more for show than anything. Anyone with a substandard IQ could get through those gates, and since she'd explained up front that it was her way or the highway, by tomorrow she planned to have an armed guard at the gate twenty-four seven.

She had spent the previous evening looking at aerial photos of the grounds as well as blueprints of the West home. According to Gary's paperwork, Tory had purchased the house a year ago and moved in six months later, after some extensive remodeling. Jolene West's bedroom was located in the northwest corner of the house on the second floor and, from where Lee was standing, was partially visible from the street. With a long-range lens or a good pair of binoculars someone could see practically anything, if they knew where to look. The incompetence angered her; these were the types of details that would no longer be overlooked.

The sound of a car slowing caught her attention. Focusing on the front gate, she observed someone wearing sunglasses and a hat straining to get a glimpse of the house from the driver's seat. Suddenly it dawned on her, a guard wouldn't be enough. The West sisters needed privacy. Fortunately for them, concealment was her specialty.

The car rolled away slowly as she raised her hand to knock again. Her knuckles barely made contact with the freshly painted wood before the door swung open and an athletic-looking brunette in high heels and a French braid admitted Lee with a sweep of her hand.

"You must be Lee. Nice to meet you. I'm Marilyn," she said, extending her hand.

"Ma'am."

Lee returned the firm handshake, glancing briefly at the beautiful woman who stood just a few inches shy of her own six feet. The three-inch heels accentuated the long muscular legs below the woman's short maroon skirt, evidence of many hours of intense bike riding, which substantiated Gary's profile that Marilyn Stockard had at one time been a semi-pro bike rider, until a devastating knee injury took her out of contention. Now she was Tory West's manager, the person behind the scenes who made sure every aspect of Tory's career fell into place.

Lee stepped into the foyer and studied the spacious living room to the left of the large entryway. Unfortunately, the inside of the home appeared to be as inviting as the outside. *Jesus, this place is more open than a public park. Privacy shades need to be installed over the windows. That chair near the front window—gone.*

"Would you please follow me," Marilyn said, escorting Lee to the first door on the left. "Have a seat. Miss West will be with you shortly. Can I get you something to drink?"

"No, thank you, ma'am. And if it's all the same to you, I'd rather stand."

"Of course."

Lee paced in a tight line, another nervous habit she'd picked up since returning from war. Looking around her, she studied the eccentrically furnished office. Two uncomfortable-looking high-back chairs sat in front of a gas fireplace to her left. An antique mahogany desk to her right sat on top of a snow-white rug. Awards covered the entire far wall, everything from the group's most recently won Grammys to the newest edition, Record of the Year. The office was devoid of any style or personal touches, and as she was about to go look for Marilyn to see what was taking so long, in walked the lead singer of Total Femme, Tory West.

"Lee, nice to meet you. I'm Tory."

Lee returned the handshake firmly. "Ma'am, it's a pleasure."

Tory's laugh was deep and hearty. "All you ex-military types are the same. I've worked with enough of you to know."

"Ma'am?"

"My name is Tory, and just to clarify, if you call my sister Jolene *ma'am*, no amount of military training will prepare you for the verbal assault you'll get."

Lee kept her expression neutral. She didn't care what others thought of her, nor was she being paid to win a popularity contest. Truthfully, she didn't plan to be seen much at all. Her job was to stand in the shadows and protect when necessary, and that's what she planned to do. "I'll try and remember that. Thanks for the warning."

"No problem." Tory sat behind her desk and motioned for Lee to sit opposite her. "Gary tells me that you're the best at what you do. Is that true?"

The question was simple enough, but how could she answer it honestly? She'd been the best at one time, but her job duties in the service had differed somewhat from those required of a full-time babysitter for some rich woman's sister. What she'd never tell Tory West was that she was terrified of being responsible for another person's life again. In the service, she had been required to give the right orders to keep her men alive. The last order she'd given had killed them all. But, all in all, she didn't know too many people with her skills, and this job would give her something to focus on other than the screams that twisted her dreams and the smell of burning flesh that haunted her days, so she answered the only way she could. "Yes, ma'am."

"Good." Tory nodded. "Because I need the best, Lee. My sister's protection means everything to me. Has Gary filled you in on all the details?"

"Yes, he has. But may I ask if she's more willing to accept the protection since he and I last talked?"

"No." Tory sounded exasperated. "But she also doesn't understand what's good for her. Since I do, and she's in no position to fight me right now, I talked her into one bodyguard, and you're it."

Lee nodded, even though she still didn't like the situation. "Did Gary also explain my stipulations?"

"Yes. And I have to tell you, I'm not used to being told what I will and won't do, especially in my own home."

"I understand that, but you have to trust me to know what's best for your sister's protection."

"And that means…"

"It means that since she lives in this house, I expect certain things to be done that might interfere with your life too. You have to understand that the measures I take will keep you safe as well, but as long as we agree that I have *her* best interest in mind, I'm sure it won't be too much of a problem, considering you told me that her protection means everything."

"You do get to the point," Tory said, apparently considering Lee's words. "Anything I should know about now?"

"No, ma'am. I'll give Gary a list when I speak to him."

"Very well. Then before we go over the financial details, I'd like you to meet my sister."

"Of course."

Following Tory West, Lee ascended the ornate spiral staircase and used the time to study the woman guiding her. The superstar looked nothing like the person on the album and magazine covers that Gary had shared with her yesterday. In fact, with her long blond hair and Armani business suit, she looked more like she spent her days as a CEO for a multi-million-dollar corporation than as the lead singer for an all-female leather band. Her initial assessment of the singer had been correct. Tory West's stage persona was entirely a façade.

They arrived at the second-story landing, making a left to travel in the opposite direction of the multi-level library. They stopped in front of the last door at the end of the hallway and Tory knocked.

"Jo, it's me. I brought company."

"Come in."

The first thing Lee noticed when entering Jolene West's bedroom was the king-sized bed engulfing the woman lying in its center, surrounded by thick pillows and covered with a plush down comforter. All it took was a quick glance to determine that even with the injuries to Jolene's face, she was attractive. Even though the lacerations helped her tell them apart, Lee would be able to tell instantly who was who just by their demeanor. Where Tory radiated a calm and controlled nature, the energy vibrating from her sister was equivalent to a firecracker on the verge of exploding. Jolene had her arms folded across her chest, her body tense and her mouth set in a hard frown. From the look of contempt on the young woman's face, she wasn't happy to see Lee and didn't have a problem expressing her displeasure.

Tory sat next to Jolene on the bed and motioned Lee closer. "Jo, this is Lee Winters. Lee, this is my sister, Jolene West."

Jo stared at the new bodyguard, soaking in the appearance of the tall, dark-eyed woman with the wavy brown hair. Lee Winters wasn't anything like the rest of Tory's shadows, but then again she wouldn't be, since all of Tory's bodyguards were men. Lee wore a plain black T-shirt stretched tight over her muscled chest, displaying a soft swell of breasts. Her arms were well sculpted and her triceps bulged against the taut material. She could almost discern Lee's six-pack abs through the cotton of her shirt. Her black Levi's were form-fitting and showed every muscle in her thighs. The disheveled haircut made her look a lot younger than her thirty-two years, a fact she knew from the resume Tory had given her. Her eyes were as dark as fine coffee beans and just as potent. A thick red scar resembling a dragon's tail coiled around her arm and disappeared into her sleeve. But what completely made Jo's heart speed up a few pleasant notches were the black Tony Lama boots, complete with silver tips. Man, she'd always been a sucker for nice cowboy boots.

"Ma'am," Lee said, extending her hand.

Jo couldn't tell if it was the unexpected softness of Lee Winter's hand or the fact that she'd just called her *ma'am* that caused her to recoil, but she was instantly irritated. "Let's get something straight. That *ma'am* crap stops right now. No need for formality. The name's Jo."

Lee nodded, her expression never wavering. "I'll consider it."

"The hell you will." Jo couldn't believe the woman's nerve. She'd die before she allowed Lee to follow her around calling her *ma'am* or *Ms. West* all day. She'd feel like she was in some kind of sick S-and-M game. She turned to face Tory, who apparently found the exchange amusing. "Tory, I don't think—"

"Thank you, Lee," Tory said, expertly cutting Jo off. "I'll see you downstairs in a few minutes."

"Yes, ma'am," Lee said, but her focus never wavered from Jo. "See you tomorrow morning."

"Are you crazy?" Jo said as Lee exited. "I can't work with… with *that*!"

"That?"

"Yes…that!" Jo said, pointing at the door. "She's like a damn robot. You need to find me someone else." Jo threw the covers off and attempted to stand, but grimaced as the crippling pain shot down her leg and she fell back onto the bed.

"Jo, don't."

"Damn it. Let me go!"

Lee raced back through the door. "Is everything all right?"

"Fine. Just fucking great!" Jo grunted, slapping Tory's hands away.

Jo collapsed back into the pillows and saw Lee scrutinizing her every move. Lee had an intense look on her face, and even though Tory was there with them, that intensity was focused solely on her. She'd never been in a room with *anyone* who blatantly ignored Tory. The thought intrigued her.

Studying Lee closely, Jo could see why Gary had picked her for the job. A daunting presence at almost six feet tall, with broad shoulders and a trim waist, Lee was the picture of strength and conviction. Her stiff posture and piercing dark eyes made her look like someone who was ready for battle, who could take on an army with her bare hands. But something in her steady gaze brought Jo up short. Was it curiosity or something else? "I thought you'd left?"

"I was waiting for your sister at the other end of the hall when it sounded like you may have needed my assistance, but I was obviously mistaken. See you tomorrow."

Jo studied the retreating form, wondering what could have made Lee appear so uncomfortable. She couldn't imagine what would make a woman of Lee's caliber uneasy. "Who is this woman, Tor? And don't tell me she's just some average military grunt, because ever since you met Gary, I've met enough of them to know. I read her file. It had about as much information as my driver's license."

"Gary made me promise—"

"Save it. Tell me or she's gone."

"All right. Supposedly she's some type of retired army sergeant who was the only woman ever to be accepted into the Ranger program."

"A *Ranger*? What happened?"

"All Gary would tell me was that she was injured in the line of duty and discharged before she had a chance to enter the program."

"That's it? They just let her go?"

"As far as I know." Tory handed Jo two Percocet and a glass of water. "Now here, take this."

"But—"

"No *buts*. Take it."

Jo swallowed the pills, sighing as she collapsed back into the pillows. "There's more you're not telling me."

The look in Tory's eyes softened and she brushed a stray lock of hair out of Jo's eyes. "She comes highly recommended. This isn't some recruit fresh out of the service. She's the best of the best. She can protect you and will at any cost, even to her own safety. Don't you see," Tory said, placing Jo's hand over her heart, "I only want the *best* for you."

Jo nearly said "since when" but refrained. She appreciated all Tory was doing for her, but she couldn't wait to heal so she could get out of this damn house and on with her life. "Fine. But like I said before, after I'm healed, I'm outta here."

"Thank you."

Jo shrugged. "Don't get too carried away. GI Jane still might not make it through tomorrow. Oh, and by the way, if she calls me *ma'am* one more time, Ms. Rules and Regulations better understand the concept of retreat before I really go postal."

Tory laughed but Jo didn't find the situation funny. If Lee Winters continued to infuriate her, all the training in the world wouldn't protect Lee from her wrath.

❖

The sun was just beginning to set as Lee stretched out on her reclining deck chair and listened to the sounds of the traffic below. A little more than a day ago, she'd stood here contemplating suicide. She hadn't had a focus and saw no way out. Funny how much had changed in so little time.

As she sat there, sipping her favorite tequila, she thought about her new job and the woman she'd promised to protect. Now she had a purpose, a duty. In the service, duty and honor had meant everything to her. She had sworn to protect, defend. She put up barriers so nothing got in the way of that duty and kept them up when she got out. She'd been shielding her own pain for a long time and knew all too well the demons she'd have to face if her walls came crumbling down. Her training helped keep those walls in place and assured her those barriers were always impenetrable, because without them, the remainder of her sanity would disperse like the desert sands that had begun the process. She knew plenty of people who had come back mentally less than whole, and they were the ones who had allowed their barriers to drop just long enough for the demons to escape and ravage what was left of their humanity.

Having something to occupy her time definitely made her feel useful again. She had a reason to get up in the morning, to live. Something to look forward to instead of waking to the nightmares and reliving the collage of painful images throughout her waking moments. But more important, she could apply the skills she'd been trained to use. This job could be more than an opportunity to babysit. It was a chance to get a part of her life back on track, a way to dim the pain of losing the chance to be one of the army's elite combat operatives, a dream that the same bomb that killed her men had shredded.

Her thoughts drifted back to Jolene West. *Jo*, she corrected herself. The feisty blonde was a combination of fire and ice, a trait she found unusual, yet intriguing. She couldn't see too many people getting the best of her, but since someone had, she would make sure it never happened again.

The photos Gary had provided of Jo didn't do her beauty justice. She was much more captivating in person. Uneasiness settled over her as she pictured the damage done to Jo's body. The cuts on Jo's face were numerous but not deep, although a few would probably scar. Then there was the cast that had protruded from the sheets and the taped ribs she'd glimpsed when the two sisters were struggling. Jo's accident might have left her temporarily incapacitated, but nothing seemed to have dampened her spirit. If she was going to protect Jo, she'd have to stay one step ahead of her and the person who'd tried to do her harm. Odds were that Jo would never have to worry about being attacked again because the stalker was only using Jo as a means to get to Tory. But fortunately for Jo, she didn't play the odds or believe in luck.

She reopened the folder on the West sisters, rereading every piece of information that Gary had provided. She would spend the next few days becoming familiar with her surroundings and Jo's habits. The more she knew about Jo and the workings of the household, the easier it would be for her to do her job. Even the tiniest details could be critical if something were to happen. And if Jo was as unpredictable and hard-headed as she seemed, Lee would need to be prepared for just about anything.

Before Lee left the house, Tory explained that Jo wouldn't be able to go out much except for doctor's appointments during the next few weeks. What she didn't know and forgot to ask at the time was why. This was just one reason why working with civilians was difficult for her. According to a copy of Jo's medical records that Gary had someone dig up, Jo's injuries, although serious, weren't life threatening. Her military experience had taught her that broken bones and concussions shouldn't keep someone from going anywhere for weeks at a time. A few days maybe, but after their brief introduction that morning, she doubted much could keep Jo from doing anything she set her mind to. She hoped she would be granted a few days to get a feel for Jo and her routines. Not knowing anything about Jo made her edgy, but if the spirited blonde she met this morning became livelier as she healed, Lee's skills would soon be tested in more ways than one.

Jo still had weeks of recovery in store for her, and the thought of the pain she'd have to endure pulled at Lee's heart, surprising her. She couldn't remember a time she'd allowed herself to become emotionally involved with a job or a task that needed to be completed, and she couldn't allow that to happen now. Experiencing emotions on a personal level bothered her because she didn't know how to categorize them in her orderly life. No sense in worrying about it. It had never happened before, so it wouldn't happen now.

Studying the psychological profile on the stalker, she became increasingly irritated with the amount of vague information.

Name: Unidentified Subject
Age: Approx. twenty-five to thirty-five years old
Sex: High Probability Male
Race: High Probability Caucasian

Profile: UNSUB most likely is a loner and has access to ample resources. He is knowledgeable and highly resourceful. Excellent at covering tracks. No prints left at crime scene or on letters. Subject is unstable and extremely volatile.

Levels of Stalking:
Behavioral analysis suggests UNSUB has progressed through four stages of stalker identity:

Stage One: Attraction Phase
Stalker has made contact by e-mail, texts, or phone calls. He has claimed his love for the victim and made his intentions for that love known. His attraction to the romantic interest probably occurred within a few minutes of first meeting. The attraction is completely physical, with disregard for all personality differences. The subject will usually have unrealistic fantasies about a

relationship with the love interest and typically assigns unrealistic qualities to his object of affection. The beginnings of obsessive, controlling behaviors begin to manifest.

As she rifled through the notes, she realized that the stalker had reached this phase approximately two months ago, when the letter-writing had first started. Whatever had triggered his psychotic break must have happened during this two-month period of time. She'd get Gary to look into all those possible avenues tomorrow, everything from events the Total Femme star had attended to parties thrown at the house. Someone close to her had to know this whack job, and they needed to find that person quickly before he caused any more harm.

Stage Two: Anxious Phase
Stalker begins to exhibit an escalation in controlling, obsessive behaviors. An illusion of intimacy is created by the afflicted person regardless of the other person's true feelings. The need to stay in contact with their love interest by any means escalates, such as letters, texts, phone calls, etc. They begin to exhibit strong feelings of mistrust. Violent reactions, whether physical or verbal, are directed toward object of affection or oneself. This becomes worse as obsessive demands aren't met.

According to the file, Tory had never received a text, e-mail, or phone call of any kind, so the increased number of letters over the past few weeks made sense. It also explained why the letters had become more demanding, more violent. The more she refused him, the angrier he was bound to become.

Stage Three: Obsessive Phase
This phase is marked by the subject beginning to lose total control and suffering from extreme anxiety. They think about their love interest nonstop, developing a rapid escalation in behaviors

such as phone calls, letters, etc. Subject may accuse love interest of infidelity and perform drive-bys of home or other places where person may spend time.

Lee thought about the person she had witnessed driving by the West home earlier that day, and a sick feeling in the pit of her stomach emerged. From tomorrow on, around-the-clock cameras would be posted at every available angle right outside the front gate. If he attempted to drive by again, maybe they would get a good look at his face, or at the very least a license plate. She wouldn't go home tomorrow until the task was completed.

Stage Four: Destructive Phase
The final phase is the most dangerous of the four phases. At this point the stalker is in a deep depression and will most likely display feelings of self-blame or self-hatred. A desire to seek revenge is likely. Suicidal thoughts may manifest, as may thoughts of homicide.

"What does that mean exactly?" she murmured in irritation. A physical confrontation? A break-in? Damn it. She needed specifics. Gary was usually good at his job, but this piece of paper was sloppy work. For all she knew, he could have found out this information himself by Googling stalkers over the Internet. She'd call him first thing in the morning and double-check to make sure his source was legit. Knowing Gary, if he had a source it would probably be a current or ex-FBI profiler, although the credentials didn't matter as long as the information was accurate.

She had already laid out three pairs of pressed black jeans and matching T-shirts for the week, along with the nine-millimeter Beretta she was licensed to carry. After cleaning her weapon and polishing her boots, she would be equipped for the next few days. Following her motto, "It pays to be prepared," she wouldn't let anyone catch her off guard or not be ready in a moment's notice.

She dimmed the light above her head to a soft glow, then burrowed under the sheets and tried to relax. She still couldn't sleep soundly throughout the night, and when her demons surfaced, it was easier to wake up to the light than to night's shadows. As the heaviness of sleep overtook her, she pictured Jo's face and drifted off to sleep with a smile.

CHAPTER FIVE

What do you mean she's gone?" Tory said as Marilyn handed her a copy of the upcoming tour schedule. When Jo hadn't met her for breakfast at seven, Tory had sent Marilyn upstairs to look for her. Since then, Marilyn had scoured the house from top to bottom, but they still hadn't found any sign of her. "She's not supposed to leave the damn house."

"You know Jo." Marilyn shrugged. "She probably needed fresh air and went for a walk. I'm sure she's fine."

Tory threw the schedule onto the desk, the papers slapping against the polished wood. "A walk? Listen to yourself? She's on crutches and has broken ribs, for God's sakes!"

"Tory, calm down."

"No, you calm down and find my sister!" Tory picked up the phone to call Gary just as Dan Powers, her primary bodyguard, appeared with Lee Winters in tow. "Oh, thank God, you're here. Jo's missing."

Lee stopped. She couldn't have heard correctly. Two minutes on the job and already Jo was missing? "For how long?" she asked calmly, although she felt like punching something.

"We don't know. Last time I saw her was around ten last night."

Lee chastised herself inwardly for already dropping the ball. A good soldier was always prepared for anything, which just proved she wasn't a hundred percent on her game. After scribbling down a few notes, she handed the piece of paper to Dan. "Call Gary and assemble the rest of the guys. We'll meet in five to do a full sweep of the house and grounds."

Dan nodded but glanced in Tory's direction. She answered his unspoken question. "I told you, whatever she says, goes."

Lee turned her attention back to Tory. "What was the last thing you two talked about?"

"What we always talk about. Her leaving. She was angry and we fought, but I didn't think she'd actually leave."

"When did you realize she was gone?"

"About a half hour ago."

"Seven thirty," Lee said, mostly to herself, as she looked at her watch. "And you checked her room thoroughly?"

"Of course! I'm not stupid, just upset." Tory inhaled deeply in an obvious attempt to rein in her temper. "I'm sorry, that was rude. Yes, Marilyn checked."

"My apologies but I have to cover everything. Has she ever done this before?"

"Unfortunately." This time when Tory spoke, the angry edge was gone, replaced with resigned weariness. "Jo is very independent and doesn't enjoy being told what to do. She promised me last night that if she left the grounds she'd tell someone. It's not like she could go far in her condition so I didn't think much of it. Besides, she promised we'd talk and have breakfast together before I left today. It's not something we're able to do when I'm touring. The nights turn into days faster than I'd like when we're on the road."

Lee didn't want to frighten Tory, but there was a nine-hour gap between when Tory had last seen Jo and the time she realized Jo was missing. Anything could have happened during that period. She could have wanted some time alone, or she could have been kidnapped. Lee jotted down every detail Tory could remember, from what Jo was wearing to what she ate for her last meal. She ignored the slight tremor in her hand. Coffee on an empty stomach always made her a little shaky.

"Shouldn't you be out looking for her or something?" Tory said. "I don't understand all these questions. Who cares about her eating and sleeping habits? She's missing and you need to find her!"

Lee rested her hip against the desk, not taking the outburst personally. Mentally detaching herself from other people's emotions had always been one of her gifts. She couldn't think about what would happen if another person she was asked to protect died. So she focused on the list of tour dates on Tory's desk to concentrate on something other than Tory's emotional state. "Ma'am, the details are important because they allow me to outline a pattern of your sister's behavior. According to what you've told me, this is not the first time she's—"

"What's going on?" Jo asked from the doorway, leaning heavily on her crutches.

"What's wrong?" Tory asked angrily. "Where the hell have you been? I've been worried sick!"

"I needed some air," Jo said, her tone defensive. "And since when do I have to check in with you?"

"Damn it, Jo. You know you don't have to check in, but with everything going on didn't you think I'd be worried? All I ask is that you tell someone—me, your bodyguard, anyone here— that you're going out. You're still injured. Something could have happened to you."

"And that doesn't sound like checking in to you? Tell someone. Leave a note. Being chained to a goddamned bodyguard!"

"Look, I don't want to argue."

"Then stop telling me what the hell to do. I went for a walk, Tory. A walk!" Jo said, her voice escalating with each word. "What do you want me to do? Sit in bed all day and play solitaire?"

Lee watched the sisters argue but stayed out of the way. They reminded her of two billy goats, fighting for space on a steep cliff. Jo's defensive posture and the flaring of her nostrils were sure signals that the final blow would be delivered shortly. Jo might have only gone for a walk, but she did so by escaping the notice of the four bodyguards currently on duty. After today she would make damn sure it never happened again.

"No, I didn't expect you to lock yourself away, but why can't you understand—" Tory paused as Jo swayed and fainted. "Jo!"

Lee leapt forward and caught Jo's head before it hit the ground. Placing two fingers on Jo's carotid artery, she detected the even pulsations against her fingertips. Her own heartbeat steadied as Jo slowly opened her eyes.

"Lee?"

"Yes." *Good, she's talking and aware of her surroundings.* "Are you okay?"

"I think so," Jo murmured. She placed her hands on Lee's forearms and tightened her grip. "Help me up." Jo made it halfway to her feet before she sagged again, but this time Lee was ready. She held her close, taking her weight to keep her from further injuring herself.

"Jo, honey," Tory said, holding her sister's face between her hands.

"Ms. West," Lee said to Tory as she cradled Jo's head and hooked one arm under Jo's legs, lifting her as easily as she would a small child. "Move."

Lee carried Jo up the stairs, being careful not to bump her casted leg against any obstacles along the way. She placed Jo onto her bed, ignoring the fatigue in her left arm, more concerned with Jo's incoherent murmurs and the glazed expression that suggested she was still disoriented. She tried to adjust pillows and blankets to make Jo comfortable, while Tory stood next to the bed talking into her cell phone.

"Yes, Doctor. Twice. No. Yes…uh hum…yes. Okay…thank you. See you soon. Bye." Tory sat on the edge of the bed and held Jo's hand. "Dr. Chase says you're to stay put until he arrives. He told me to give you fluids and ask if you've had any troubles with your vision or if your headache has returned."

"Tory," Jo said, her voice stronger but still weary. "I'm not an invalid. When the doctor gets here, I'll talk to him. Now, please, everyone out."

Tory left without another word. Lee, though, remained rooted to the foot of the bed, studying Jo like a terrain map, searching for any signs of weakness or confusion that could mean trouble.

Jo glanced at Lee curiously. "Why are you still here?"

"Just leaving. I'll be on the other side of the door if you need anything. Hope you feel better."

"Outside my *door*? Why?"

"Because that's my job. Call out if you need anything."

Lee closed the door behind her and stared at her hands, willing them to stop shaking. The dark circles under Jo's eyes and her fainting spell had her worried, and until the doctor arrived and supplied a more clinical update, she wouldn't be able to relax or calm her racing heart.

❖

Dr. Chase closed Jo's bedroom door and nearly bumped into Tory, who was pacing in the hallway. Lee remained leaning against the wall close enough to overhear their hushed conversation.

"How is she, Doctor? Is she okay? Does she need to go back to the hospital? Is she—"

"Whoa! Easy. She's fine. The dizziness was most likely due to hypoglycemia, since she told me she hasn't eaten much in the past few days. Not eating combined with the little bit of exercise from her walk and the pain medication wasn't a good mix. I tried to tell her that before," he said, and chuckled. "But you know Jo. Luckily she fainted inside the house rather than outside by herself."

He'd been with Jo an hour. A very long hour, in Lee's opinion. Finally, she could take a deep breath, but not until Tory and the doctor were elsewhere. She remained motionless with her hands in her pockets and her back against the wall. If her dark clothes didn't stand out against the white walls, no one would have even noticed she was there.

"Thank you, Doctor," Tory said. "God, she's so damn stubborn!" Tory was speaking to the air more than anything. The doctor nodded and gave instructions about bed rest and food before he left.

"Sure seems that way," Lee said, realizing immediately she'd spoken out loud.

"Starting to regret taking this job?"

"Not at all. But until she accepts the idea of needing a bodyguard, she could be in danger."

"I agree. Can I ask a favor?"

Lee motioned warily for Tory to continue.

"Jo won't listen to me. In fact, she's barely speaking to me. Maybe you could get through to her. Make her understand."

"I don't think—"

"Please, Lee." Tory stepped closer and lowered her voice in an obvious attempt to make sure Jo couldn't hear them through the door. "I need her to appreciate that this isn't a joke."

"Ms. West. This isn't a good idea." *And definitely not my expertise.*

"Probably not," Tory said, and smiled. "But I have nothing to lose."

Tory placed her back against the wall and hunched her shoulders, a telltale sign of defeat. From what little she'd witnessed of the superstar's controlling personality, she had to be at her wits' end to be reduced to begging. It further confirmed her suspicions that no matter how strained the sisters' relationship was, Tory was willing to do whatever it took to protect Jo. It wasn't what she signed up for, but if it kept her client safe, she was willing to give it a go.

"I'll speak to her if you think it will help."

"Thank you."

Yeah, right. She'd need more than thanks to get through Jo's wall of independence.

❖

Jo rolled over with a groan, her back protesting from lying in the same position for the last few hours. She swallowed, her throat as dry as sandpaper from falling asleep with her mouth open. The water glass was inches beyond her grasp. Maybe if she could get just a little closer…

"Ow, shit." She grimaced as her cast leg tumbled awkwardly to the floor, pulling her halfway off the bed. The death grip she had on the covers was the only thing keeping her from sliding all the way to the floor. "Help!"

Lee burst through the door, her gun at the ready, and quickly scanned the room, to find Jo half hanging out of bed. She holstered her firearm, carefully picked up the casted leg, and placed it gently back onto the bed.

"Can I get you anything for the pain?" Lee asked, her voice laced with concern.

"No, but thanks. I'm actually feeling better now that I'm not engaged in a sadistic version of Twister."

"Are you sure? Maybe something for that headache?"

"What makes you think I have a headache?"

Lee smiled. "Educated guess. Besides, I've been told I'm one helluva good detective."

Jo bet she was good at a lot of things but couldn't think about any of those *things* right now, especially with Lee staring at her so intently. She was acutely aware of the fact she was only wearing panties and a T-shirt. Her nipples and clit hardened involuntarily, a response to Lee's hand still resting on her thigh. Self-consciously she pulled the blanket up to cover her whole body before it gave her away. "You're right. It's terrible. But before I take something for it, I have to go to the bathroom. Could you…uh…possibly help me up?"

"Of course. What can I do?"

"For one, you can stand down, Soldier. Your seriousness weirds me out a bit. And then you can start by handing me my robe and those crutches."

Lee turned away to give Jo privacy as she slipped on a robe. As soon as Jo voiced the okay to turn back around, she held the crutches steady for her until she was able to maneuver on her own power.

"You don't have to follow me, you know," she said as Lee stayed close. "The bathroom is only a few feet away."

"Yes, I know. But for your safety I'd rather be nearby just in case."

"Do you always have to be so annoyingly in charge, Lee?" She hadn't meant to sound so harsh, but Lee's freakish control was starting to grate on her nerves. Tory had enough say over her life at the moment, and she wasn't about to give up any more to anyone for any reason.

Lee glanced down at her, her face a blank canvas. "Yes. But I am sorry it 'weirds you out,' as you so interestingly put it. My job is to protect you, Ms. West. So I'll wait for you here. Just in case."

Jo was too disconcerted by Lee's honest answer to respond right away. The former soldier was such a contradiction—helpful and concerned one moment, cool and remote the next. She couldn't get her bearings around her new bodyguard and needed a moment to think. "Yeah, thanks. I'll only be a minute."

She closed the bathroom door, thankful for the privacy. Figuring out her new bodyguard was like navigating a minefield, and she really didn't know whether she wanted to hug her or hit her. When she was finished and felt slightly more human, she returned to bed and studied Lee, composed as always, standing at the far end of the room and looking a little unsure what to do next. She could tell by the slight fidget of Lee's hand that she was a tad uneasy. She wasn't sure if Lee was aware of the nervous habit, but the thought of making her squirm just a little gave Jo a bit of satisfaction.

"How about you come and sit over here for a while?" Jo pointed to the chair by her bed. "We could get to know each other since it appears we're going to be spending a lot of time together."

"I'm good here. Thanks."

"Funny, you don't look okay. In fact you look...nervous. Like you're ready to crawl out of your skin. Do I make you uncomfortable, Lee?"

"Really, ma'am, I'm fine." Lee's body became even more rigid and her gaze hardened.

"Okay then." *It's just freaky how she can flip a switch like that. Robot.* "We haven't had a chance to talk. Come on...sit. Why don't you tell me a little about your background?"

Lee acquiesced and sat rigidly in the nearby chair. "What would you like to know?"

"Anything, I suppose. My sister told me you were in the service. How about we start there?" The sudden change that came over Lee made Jo wish she'd asked another question. Lee dropped her eyes to her hands, where they dangled between her legs. Her shoulders hunched forward, her jaw clenched. "Hey. I didn't mean to pry."

"No worries. I guess I don't talk much about those days anymore."

"I heard from Tory you were going to be a Ranger—the only woman to ever get accepted into the program."

Physically, Lee was still sitting in the chair, but mentally her barren gaze screamed she was a thousand miles away. Jo had no idea if Lee was even aware of her hands balled into fists, but the sudden stiffness in her body suggested that a thick barrier existed around the subject, which made Jo want to dig deeper to discover her secrets.

"That was my plan, but it didn't work out."

"Sorry. Can I ask what stopped you?"

"Ms. West—"

"Enough with that already," Jo said in exasperation. "Look, I understand you have a job to do, but that *job* involves me. I don't understand all the formality. Why can't we get to know each other? You know...like friends."

"Ma'am, I don't need friends, but I would appreciate your cooperation."

"My cooperation." *Yeah, like that would ever happen.* "Oh, I get it. You want me to be a good girl to make your cushy babysitting job easier."

"No. That's not what I meant."

"Then what did you mean?"

Lee stood, obviously intent on putting distance between them. Tory used a similar tactic when she was about to say something Jo wasn't going to like. "Since we're going to be spending a lot of time together, I would appreciate if you took the protection seriously. Maybe we can even come to some kind of agreement—"

"Stop. Did Tory send you in here to give me this little pep talk?"

"Yes. But she was only thinking of you."

"I don't give a shit what Tory was thinking. Jesus! First my sister, and now you. You all need to get off my back. Protect me... fine. From what or who while I'm cooped up in this house, I don't know. I suppose the boogeyman could be in my closet."

"Not possible. I already checked."

"A sense of humor." Jo smiled and her shoulders relaxed slightly. "I underestimated you."

"You're not the first one to say that to me. But seriously, my job is to keep you safe."

"And that means what exactly?"

"That *means* I'm your shadow. Where you go—I go."

Jo sighed and was suddenly very tired. The John Wayne routine was running thin, but the pill she'd taken was starting to kick in and she could barely keep her eyes open. "I understand," she said with a yawn. "Now sit and tell me why you aren't a Ranger. Or do you really think I didn't catch you changing the subject?"

Lee returned to her chair and held Jo's steady gaze. The barriers were still there, but a flicker of something else in Lee's eyes hinted at vulnerability. "I was injured and released from duty."

Even though Jo knew very little about Lee, their brief exchange made her sure of one thing. Lee Winters didn't do anything halfway. She'd obviously been the best to even have been considered for the Ranger program, and her injuries had to have been substantial for her to have lost that chance. The thought of that loss and the pain she must have endured saddened Jo. "But you're okay now, right?"

"I'm fine. But you should get some rest. I'll see you in the morning."

"Wait!"

"Yes?"

"I wanted to thank you. You know. For helping me earlier."

Lee glanced over her shoulder and smiled. "You're welcome. Good night."

Jo sank back into the pillows as Lee closed the door behind her. She was exhausted from a mixture of their conversation and the pill she'd taken earlier and was glad for the moment of peace. Closing her eyes she drifted off, eventually falling asleep while imagining strong arms wrapped around her in a secure and comforting embrace.

CHAPTER SIX

Lee leaned against the open balcony doors of her apartment, studying the angry mass of grayish-black clouds that cluttered the eerie night sky. Absently twirling the amber liquid inside her glass, she knew she'd already begun to fall victim to the calming effects of Don Julio's best tequila. She needed the intervention more often this past year to help her sleep. If sleep continued to elude her, the hallucinations she'd suffer from would be worse than her nightmares. All she was really doing was trading one demon for another. But this was definitely the lesser of two evils.

Particles of debris swirled through the air, a sure sign of the impending storm. The cool, powerful gusts helped dry the sweat that had accumulated on her cotton T-shirt during her evening run, the exercise a necessity to get her back into the type of shape she was accustomed to. Diligence was the key to her success in life. Routine gave her the ability to push past the pain and accept any challenge that she needed to face. The loss of both of those things had nearly led her to an early grave. Now that she had a reason to get up every day, she felt like she had her feet back under her once more.

Two weeks had passed since she'd shared a few private minutes alone with Jo. Since then they'd barely spoken. There had been a few hellos here and there, but Jo rarely left the confines of her house, or her room, for that matter. Lee had used the free time to get acquainted with the other bodyguards and gain a better sense of the layout and routine of the occupants and staff of the West home.

Security cameras had been installed the day after Jo's Houdini routine. Tory had actually protested at first, saying they were unnecessary, but all it took was for Lee to point out how easily Jo had escaped everyone's notice and that it wouldn't be all that difficult for someone else to gain access to the grounds. Security guards had been hired to man the front gate, which caused another commotion. Lee explained, again, that if the sisters were adamant about maintaining as much privacy as possible, certain security measures would be necessary. Tory finally conceded after a lengthy discussion, but she clearly wasn't entirely convinced. She felt having Lee as Jo's personal body guard should be all that was necessary, and while Lee was glad Tory had so much faith in her, she pointed out that she wasn't in the house twenty-four hours a day.

There'd been no further incidents with the stalker since she'd taken the job—no letters, no calls or contact of any kind. It would be nice to think he'd given up on stalking Tory, faded into the woodwork, and found someone else to occupy his time. But after reading everything available about stalkers, Lee was sure it would only be a matter of time before he surfaced and contacted Tory again.

Gary had been subdued the last few times she'd spoken with him. He kept his answers brief, which was fine with her as long as she was getting all the information necessary to do the job effectively. His emotional state worried her though, especially since his distraction most likely had to do with Tory. He was the only family she had left, a brother of sorts. They'd served together, seen death daily, survived when no one else had. They both had to live with those demons, but her job now was to make sure nothing got in the way of Jo's protection. If his focus was compromised in any way, it could put Jo's life in unnecessary danger.

People began to scurry around on the streets below as the rain picked up in intensity. She could hear quarter-sized raindrops slapping the pavement, which reminded her that a few weeks ago the ominous scene playing out in front of her would have matched her mood. But since then her life had changed considerably. She tried focusing on another one of Gary's reports, but the pages might as well have been blank. This lapse of attention still scared her, especially since Jo had become her responsibility. She was almost obsessive with every detail of a mission. Missteps of any kind were unacceptable, and she couldn't live with herself if something happened to Jo on her watch. Eight hours of rest, a well-rounded exercise program, and eating right would be her modus operandi until her job was complete. Her only indulgence, every now and then, was the small glass of liquor that offered temporary comfort and warmth.

True, human comfort was an indulgence she'd rather have for the exact same reasons. She missed the feeling of a warm body below her, the touch of another on her skin. She wanted to let go with someone, to fall asleep enveloped in someone else's arms. But since the night terrors would never allow that possibility, she'd allow the alcohol to help her let down her guard and relax. A good drink was the only thing during the war that she and her friends could look forward to after dealing with death and destruction all around them every day. The unique taste of spice and blue agave reminded her of better times and was the one vice she wasn't willing to let go of, because it kept the bad memories from overwhelming the good ones.

Stretching out on the sofa she closed her eyes, allowing the warming sensation to take over her mind and body. Instantly, images of Jo surfaced. She couldn't decide what was more captivating, the stylishly cut, silky blond hair or the enchanting smile that could light up a room. But what intrigued her most was that, hidden behind that fiery façade, was a potent vulnerability that drew her in. She'd like to get to know Jo better but couldn't get personal. Personal blurred boundaries. Jo would become more than just a job. Even though the thought was appealing it was also scary as hell and could never happen.

Lee jumped when the phone rang unexpectedly. Minutes seemed to have passed instead of hours but it was dark outside, so she'd clearly been lying there thinking far longer than she realized. She swore out loud at the way her heart was racing, frustrated at such skittish behavior. Edginess had never been a part of her chemical makeup until she'd returned injured from the war. The thought pissed her off. "Winters."

"Hey, buddy, it's me," Gary said. "Did I catch you at a bad time?"

Wiping the fatigue from her eyes, she checked her watch. *Midnight.* Whatever it was, it couldn't be good. "What's wrong?"

"Sorry to wake you but Tory has received another letter. She's frantic and wanted to meet with you an hour earlier tomorrow morning, if possible?"

Lee bolted to her feet, a sudden surge of adrenaline overcoming the exhaustion and effects of the alcohol. Another letter meant trouble, and no way in hell would she get to sleep without knowing everything was okay. "Forget tomorrow. Tell her I'll be there in ten minutes."

Lee pulled up in front of the West home to find Tory pacing on the front porch surrounded by two of her bodyguards. Even in the dim light, Dan Powers stood out, his rigid stance and perfectly trimmed goatee clearly marking him as more than just part of Tory's entourage. Lee hadn't been introduced to the new guard, whom she recognized thanks to a photograph Gary had given her. Amanda Franklin, the other guard watching Tory pace, was not only a new addition assigned to Tory's security, but the first female shadow Tory had ever used.

Amanda was a good three inches shorter than Lee, with curly auburn hair and deep-set hazel eyes. According to the docket Gary had given her, Amanda had spent the last four years in Naval Intelligence and was as equally skilled in acquiring information as he was. Gary saw Amanda as a potential asset in the future in case they needed information from sources even he couldn't access. But Lee had questioned how effective Amanda would be at guarding someone, since she'd spent more time behind the scenes in the military instead of engaged in actual combat. Since it wasn't her call to make because Tory wasn't her responsibility, she had to leave the decision up to Gary, even though she didn't agree with it.

Lee followed Tory into the house, and Tory gestured for Dan and Amanda to remain outside her study. She reached into her desk drawer and handed over a manila folder. Lee opened the flap, removing its contents with care.

You are mine. Mine! I watch. I wait. Yet still you refuse me. No one loves you more than I. We will be together soon. You can count on it. I will never let you go.

"What do you think?" Tory asked, visibly shaken.

"I'm no expert, but from what I've read he seems to be getting desperate. We may need some additional help, and I don't mean more bodyguards."

"You mean the police." It wasn't a question.

"Yes. But I was thinking more FBI."

"No!"

Why did that not surprise her? "Ms. West, it's the right thing to do. They have tools that Gary may not have access to—databases with criminal histories, psychologists who can tell us more about his personality. We need everything we can get our hands on, and we need it yesterday."

Tory closed her eyes and slumped in her chair, the stress of the evening apparently taking its toll on her. "Lee, my sister doesn't want a bodyguard—let alone the cops, FBI, or whoever you're suggesting—crawling all over our lives. The security cameras and security guards already irritate her. I can't push her any more than I am. You've seen her. She's feeling better every day, and we won't be able to talk her into staying in this house for much longer. If we keep tightening the reins she'll eventually break loose and I'll lose her forever. She already resents me for the attack. I can see it in her eyes every time she looks at me.

"What you probably don't know is that even though we're twins, I've always had it easier than Jo. Things like school and my talent have always come naturally to me. Jo has always had to struggle, and it kills me to see her in this condition when it should have been me. Deep down, I know she doesn't wish it was me in that bed, even though I'd take her place in a heartbeat. She hates me right now. I get it. But at least I'm certain she's safe with you, and I don't want to involve the authorities until I'm positive we don't have any other options."

For the first time since Lee had met Tory, she felt respect for her. She ran a hand through her disheveled hair, still not happy with Tory's refusal for outside help, but she could accept her reasons for now. "Very well, but you do realize until we work with people who are capable of tracking this lunatic down and stopping him, this situation may only get worse. Gary says the UNSUB—"

"UNSUB?"

"My apologizes, ma'am. UNSUB stands for unidentified subject."

"Oh, right. I keep forgetting you people talk a secret language that we civilians aren't supposed to understand. So tell me again why you think we need help. I thought Gary had everything under control?"

"I'm sure he's trying his best, but he's only one person. If this escalates any further, I'm going to strongly suggest getting the authorities involved." Tory nodded and closed her eyes, and Lee took the hint that the conversation was over for the moment. "Before I go, would you mind if I checked on your sister. I promise, I won't wake her if she's asleep."

"Of course," Tory said tiredly. "Good night."

❖

Jo was too wound up to sleep and had no excuse for her growing uneasiness. She'd been restless all evening. Not even reading about hot steamy sex in her new lesbian romance novel could hold her attention. Deciding a little tryptophan was in order, she was about to go downstairs for a glass of milk when a light knock sounded on her bedroom door. "Yes?"

"Ms. West, it's me," Lee said, peeking around the partially opened door. "Sorry to bother you but I noticed the light."

"What are you doing here this time of night? Is something wrong?"

Lee took her usual seat on the chair next to Jo's bed, staring at her in concern. "I came by to check on you before I went home. How are you feeling?"

"I'm wired and can't sleep."

"I get that way sometimes too."

"What do you do about it?"

"Have a drink." Lee smiled. "Helps me sleep like a baby."

Jo studied Lee, accepting the tidbit of information as a sign of Lee's humanity. "Maybe I'll try that."

"Not advisable with the meds. See you tomorrow."

"Wait!" Jo grabbed Lee's arm to stop her. "You never said why you're here."

Lee sighed and returned to the chair, running a hand through her hair. "I'm here because your sister has received another letter."

"Oh, no." Jo threw the covers off herself. "Where is she? Is she okay? Did he threaten—"

"Calm down," Lee said, keeping Jo from rising. "She's here. She's fine. And yes."

"Then I need to see her." Jo tried pushing Lee's hands away but was unsuccessful.

"Ma'am," Lee said gently. "Please calm down. I don't want you to reinjure yourself. Your sister is tucked away for the night. I promise you, she's in good hands."

"Fine! And I really wish you'd quit that *ma'am* stuff."

"I'll work on it. You should get some sleep."

"No, not yet," Jo said, placing her hand on Lee's forearm to stop her from rising. "Please...don't go."

"All right," Lee said. "I'll stay, but only for a little bit."

"Thank you. And I'm sorry...for pushing you."

"No harm, no foul," Lee said, her eyes softening.

"I guess I've been cooped up for so long I've forgotten how to interact with people."

"I understand."

"Somehow, I believe you do. Can I ask you a question?"

"Something tells me that you're going to ask it whether I say yes or no, so shoot."

Jo laughed. "I see you've been talking with Tory. She'd call it my inquisitive bullish nature."

"Bullish?"

"Yeah, as in Taurus the bull. My sign. Hers too, of course, but I take it more to heart. It's that stubborn, never-back-down side of me. Tends to get me into a lot of trouble. So back to my question. Why did you become a soldier?"

"I've never been asked that before," she said carefully. "I guess because I liked the order, the discipline. Everything is black or white. The gray areas are what I call the unknown and are a mystery to me. I don't particularly like mysteries or surprises."

"And you risked your life for your country, for other people." Jo watched as Lee closed her eyes and a wounded expression washed over her face. Her question had caused Lee pain, and that was the last thing she'd wanted to do. Lee had already healed from an injury bad enough to have caused her to leave the service. She didn't want to think of Lee being injured or suffering in any way. "Hey, I'm sorry," Jo said, placing her hand on top of Lee's to gain her attention. "Are you okay?"

Footsteps nearby and the sound of a door unlatching in the hall caused Lee to jump. She reached for her gun. "Hey, look at me," Jo said. "It's okay. It's probably only one of Tory's guards. Relax and tell me what's wrong."

Jo had no idea what was causing the pain that was evident in Lee's haunted eyes. She had just wanted to understand why soldiers did what they did to survive and trusted no one but each other. For whatever reason, she wanted Lee to trust her. Maybe it was because of their working relationship and all the time they would spend together. But on another level, she knew that Lee would be protecting her from harm, possibly putting her body at risk to save her life. The thought made her nauseous.

"Why all the questions, Ms. West?"

"I guess I really wanted to know if you'd seriously give your life for someone."

Lee's gaze hardened and her jaw tensed. The relaxed Lee had disappeared into the shadows, and in her place Jo was sure sat the soldier who'd laid it all on the line for country, honor, and duty. The transformation was fascinating and hot as hell. "Yes."

The intensity on Lee's face forced Jo to look down at her hands. She needed a change in topic before she turned into a pile of mush beneath that smoldering look. "So…uh…okay. Now that we got that straight. Is the letter the only reason you returned tonight?"

"The main one but I also had other concerns."

"Such as?"

"Are you always this inquisitive?"

"Yep. But you're more polite than my sister. She calls it being nosy." They both laughed. "So, are you going to practice avoidance techniques on me for the rest of the evening or answer my question?"

Lee grinned. "What are my choices again?"

Jo liked Lee's laugh. It was deep, throaty. She tried to imagine that voice when it became aroused. The thought made her insides tingle and her heart rate quicken. From what she'd observed of the former staff sergeant, Lee wasn't one to hold mundane conversations. Her willingness to open up was obviously Lee's way of lowering one barrier, if only temporarily, between them. "No choice. Spill."

Lee's smile faded and the serious expression returned. "I wanted to check and see if the property's security system was working properly during the evening. The sensors were giving us problems earlier but seem to be working fine now. They tend to be a little temperamental. It's all SOP but necessary."

"SOP. There you go using that army gibberish again. Speak English, please."

"I apologize. It stands for Standard Operating Procedure."

"It's also bullshit. But since you seem dead set on following this path, is there any way I can help?"

"Cooperation!" Lee said, raising an eyebrow. "Your sister would be shocked."

"Smart-ass," Jo said, playfully slapping Lee's arm. "And, you wish. Now stop blowing smoke and tell me why you really came back tonight."

"Honestly, the letter mainly, but I'm glad I did because your sister has just informed me of a few planned social engagements here at the house within the next few weeks. One small gathering is happening tomorrow," Lee said, clearly aggravated with the last-minute notice. "I needed a list of attendees so Gary can run basic security checks."

"Since when? Most of the people Tory invites to our home are friends or friends of the other band members. Tory's never had a problem before."

"True. But since *you* plan to attend, I'd like to know who's going to be there."

"And why do you need that information?"

"Simple. It's important for me to know everyone you come into contact with. That way I can make sure they're no threat to you."

"Stop. Yourself. Right. There." Jo's tone turned frosty. "You can't be serious?"

Lee looked at Jo like she didn't understand the question. "I believe I told you I'm very serious when it comes to your protection. I need to know the people within your physical proximity in order to maintain your safety. I thought you understood my position."

"Oh, I think I understand your position all right," Jo said, shooting into a seated position with a grimace. "You understand *this*. My personal life is mine. Period. No argument. No discussion. You're only here because I gave in to Tory's wishes until I'm healed. The protector routine is cute, but in a *private* setting consider yourself off the clock. Are we clear?"

"Ms. West…"

"Enough. I'm suddenly very tired. Dismissed, soldier."

Jo listened until she heard Lee's motorcycle fade into the night before she shucked off the covers and went in search of Tory. She needed to take her irritation out on someone so she could get her mind off her attractive but annoying bodyguard. This arrangement wasn't going to work. She needed out of Tory's crazy life before the walls closed in permanently around her.

CHAPTER SEVEN

G ary, there has to be something we can use." Lee ran her hands through her hair in frustration. She'd been up since 0400, unable to sleep since Tory had shown her the letter. Making it to Gary's small apartment before her shift started at seven, she'd asked if he could find out from one of his tech friends if the car the UNSUB had used in the accident had any traces of fingerprints or, for that matter, anything they could use to apprehend him. So far, zip.

"Nothing useful." Gary sounded equally as frustrated.

"There has to be something." She scanned the photos again, trying to commit every detail to memory. "How about tires?"

"From the reports, Goodyear All-Terrains. Standard tread."

"That's not what I asked." She pointed to a stack of files on his desk. "We need to think beyond the box. Did the tech guys find anything *in* those treads?"

"Oh." He searched through a folder and handed her another computer printout. "Says right here that techs found traces of adobe soil, Magnolia Virginiana and Baccharis Pitularis."

"Do I look like the Encyclopedia Britannica?" Lee snapped, her temper reaching its boiling point. Jo's life could depend on the tiniest detail and he was wasting precious time. "What the fuck does all that mean?"

"Sorry, sorry. And talk about not getting out much. Rude…"

"Gary!"

"Yeah…sorry…right." He typed the names into his computer. "The plants are all native species to California. Magnolia Virginiana and Baccharis Pitularis are most commonly known as the laurel tree and the coyote bush."

"Do we know what areas they grow in specifically?" Finally, a clue. If they could pinpoint a few areas where these plants thrived, they might get a handle on the UNSUB's location.

"No clue. But I'll ask around and get back to you," he said, the excitement of the chase evident in his voice.

"Right. Keep me posted. Anything else?"

"Not really. I talked to Tory shortly before you got here. Seems Jo's planning on having breakfast with a friend this morning. Besides that—"

"What?" Lee growled. "Alone?"

"I guess. But Tory said it's not a big deal. It's some friend from college…" He yelled after her but Lee was already out the door.

❖

Jo tilted her head back, enjoying the feel of the sun's rays warming her skin. The outdoor café was packed and noisy, the perfect environment to camouflage her upcoming conversation from Lee, who was sitting two tables away seemingly engrossed in *The New York Times*.

If Lee thought she was fooling Jo by pretending she was more interested in the business section of the paper than her, she was mistaken. She'd been angry when Lee refused to let her go out without a shadow, making Jo's decision to see her friend even more urgent. But, at the moment, her focus wasn't on her handsome bodyguard. She'd come to have breakfast with her friend Emily, whom she hadn't seen in almost a year. After her conversation with Lee last night and her argument with Tory that morning, she couldn't think of a better person to help her with her delicate situation. Hearing someone call her name, she glanced up to find the tall, attractive brunette weaving her way through the outdoor tables. Emily had always had a bubbly personality, but today it was being outshone by the sparkling two-carat diamond on her left ring finger.

"Hey, babe, nice rock," Jo said as Emily leaned forward to give her a hug.

"Thanks. My fiancé has excellent taste." Emily released Jo, sitting opposite her. "You look great. How are you feeling?"

"Like strangling the next person who asks me how I'm feeling."

"Not surprised." Emily laughed. "Oh, my God, it's been forever!" In her excitement, Emily gave her another tight hug, but the force of it caused Jo's ribs to protest and a groan escaped her lips. "Oh, Jo. I'm so sorry. I forgot about your ribs."

"It's okay."

"Really, Jo, I'm sorry. Are you okay?"

"Yes, now that you're not squeezing me to death." She glanced at Lee out of the corner of her eye, saw her beginning to rise, and subtly waved her off.

"Who is she?" Emily asked, looking over her shoulder.

"Who are you talking about?"

"Oh, please. I'm talking about that hot butch over there who hasn't taken her eyes off you since I sat down. The one that looks like she's ready to eat you alive."

Jo toyed with her napkin, refusing to meet Emily's gaze.

"Oh, this is going to be good!"

"Actually, no, it's not," Jo said bitterly. "She's my bodyguard."

"Your *bodyguard*?" Emily said. "I don't understand. Why do *you* need a bodyguard?"

"It's complicated." Jo motioned for the waiter. Suddenly a bloody Mary was in order.

"I see that. But that's not an answer, Jo."

"I know it's not, but it's one of the reasons I asked you here today."

"You're attracted to her."

Jo gazed curiously at Emily, forgetting all about the napkin she'd twisted into a pretzel. "No, I'm not."

"Why do you even try to lie to me?" Emily said, bending closer. "I know you better than your own sister. That woman is smokin'. In fact she's so hot she makes me want to switch teams."

A sudden and unexpected surge of jealousy coursed through Jo. It bothered her that anyone would show that type of interest in Lee. She wasn't sure what prompted the "just what I thought" look from Emily. It could have been the slight tensing of her shoulders or the destruction of the napkin in her lap, or both.

"Ooh, this just keeps getting better. Talk!"

"Nothing to say."

"Jo, you've been in an accident. Your sister is more famous than Princess Diana, and you currently have a bodyguard whose looks could melt the polar ice caps. Besides, you haven't stopped torturing that poor napkin since I sat down. I know you have something to tell me and she has *everything* to do with it. Talk."

Jo closed her eyes and started at the beginning. Once she began telling Emily the entire story she couldn't stop. The relief of getting it all out was like a weight being lifted off her chest. "And that's pretty much it."

"Wait, I still don't get it," Emily asked. "Why aren't the police involved?"

"Tory doesn't want the authorities involved. She's big on keeping our private lives private and thinks this guy is a nuisance who got lucky once. She's increased everyone's security and believes there won't be any more trouble."

"Huh." Emily twirled the water around in her glass.

"Don't 'huh' me. I hate it when you do that." Jo grabbed Emily's arm to get her to stop. "Tell me what you're thinking."

Emily chewed on her lower lip, the familiar habit suggesting Jo was in for a famous Emily lecture. "Look, I understand Tory feels guilty that this lunatic went after you, but why the bodyguard? Has he mentioned he plans to come after you again?"

"No, his interest is Tory. The new letter even said he's still waiting for her. As far as the bodyguard goes, it makes Tory feel better. She says she doesn't want to give him another chance to hurt me, just in case."

"Sorry, but I'm going to say something that might make you angry."

Jo shrugged. She already had enough people on her shit list, so what was one more? "Shoot."

"When are you ever going to see that it's always been about what Tory wants? What about you? You have needs! Tory can't expect to keep you under twenty-four-hour surveillance for the rest of your life. Why don't you go somewhere and get away from all this craziness?"

"My point exactly, which is why I needed to see you." Jo glanced at Lee and lowered her voice.

"I'm not following."

"Would you let me rent your beach house in Kauai? I know this is the busy season and all, but I'll pay you double whatever anyone else is offering you."

"Wait a sec. Of course you can use it, no matter what time of year it is, and you're not paying me a damn thing. I can see why you feel the need to get away, but are you positive it wouldn't be dangerous for you? I mean, I know I just said you can't be under surveillance forever, but still."

"I'll be fine. Besides, I'm not the one in danger. This entire situation is driving me crazy. Tory wants me to wait until I'm fully healed, which, according to my doctor, could take months. My sanity can't handle months of being under around-the-clock watch. I can't even walk out my bedroom door without Lee or one of Tory's goons following me. The other day, I was eating breakfast in the kitchen and one of Tory's guards sat across the table just staring at me. Gave me the damn creeps."

"Yuck."

"Yeah, see?"

"Jo, I get it. But why the beach house? You have the money to go anywhere."

"Privacy and familiarity." She wouldn't admit that even though she yearned for a normal life, the whole stalker situation still freaked her out a little. If Tory knew that, she'd have hired ten guards to surround Jo. "I know your housekeeper and your gardener because I've been there before. It's safe, secluded, I'm comfortable there, and I know my way around the island. Plus, it's less likely people will mistake me for Tory. When I'm healed, anyway."

"Fair enough. And what about hot and dangerous over there," she said, nodding over her shoulder at Lee. "Think she'll let you get away without insisting on protection?"

Jo didn't need to look at Lee to know what Emily was talking about. She sensed Lee watching her, that inscrutable gaze caressing her skin like a cool breeze on a warm summer's day. She looked away and didn't respond.

"You see what I see, don't you?"

"Don't know what you're talking about."

"Whatever! I'd have to imagine that breaking into Fort Knox would be easier than getting away from the likes of her." She pretended to shiver and wiggled her eyebrows suggestively.

"She won't have a choice. She's hired help, and I can fire her. Period. So how soon will it be available?"

"I'll check the calendar when I get home, but it should be free in about a month. Will that be good for you?"

A month more of this? Damn. "It'll have to be."

"And how do you think Tory will take the news?"

"She'll hate it but she won't have a choice." Jo fought back the tears and the burning lump in her throat. "She just can't accept that I need to move on. I'm tired of fighting with her. I love her more than she'll ever know, but I need a chance at a life without her influence and she doesn't understand that. Maybe after a little time apart, we can find a way to be close again."

Emily sighed and sat back. "I understand, but with all this stalker talk, you will be careful, right?"

"I will. Promise."

"Okay, then. I'll see what I can do."

❖

Lee watched Jo lean forward to whisper into Emily Wallace's ear. From what Gary could gather at the last minute regarding the former college friend, Emily Wallace had graduated at the top of her class in Women's Studies at UC Berkeley and was engaged to be married to the current head of the Astrophysics Department at Stanford University. Apparently she and Jo were nothing more than friends. Oddly, that left Lee with a sense of relief she didn't want to analyze.

Whatever they had been talking about, it was making Jo nervous, evident by the way she constantly twirled a stray lock of hair around her fingers. Even though their conversation was none of her business, not knowing what was increasing the stress lines around Jo's laser blue eyes was driving her crazy.

Lee radioed for their driver just as Emily rose to hug Jo good-bye. She waited for Jo by the exit, unable to hide her surprise when Jo suggested catching a matinee before heading home.

"Are you sure that's a good idea?" Lee said, concerned by Jo's evident fatigue.

"What's wrong, don't like Hugh Jackman?"

"Who's Hugh Jackman?" Lee asked curiously.

"Who's Hugh Jackman? You know, Wolverine."

"Not particularly. I've seen enough action in my life so I don't need to watch it too. Besides, I haven't seen a movie in years. Don't like sitting that long unless I'm doing something productive." Lee opened the car door for Jo, waiting as she scooted across the seat.

"But you sit or stand all the time and do nothing. I know, I see you. Out in the hallway or like today while we ate lunch."

"And I see you," Lee said, sliding in next to Jo, their thighs barely touching. "Which means I'm being very productive and doing my job."

Jo trembled on the seat, her hand visibly shaking where it rested on her thigh. Lee attributed it to the fatigue Jo must be feeling after being out for the first time in nearly a month.

"Well, you're in for a treat then. Since it seems you have to accompany me *wherever* I go, I'm sure you'll love this movie."

Damn, this wasn't how she'd thought the rest of the afternoon would pan out. Jo needed a nap, not to go to a movie where the possibilities of an attack were endless. How was she going to protect her properly? She had no schematics of the theater. She hadn't had time to check out possible evacuation routes, employee profiles, or the size of the theater in which Jo would be sitting. That was why she needed a detailed briefing every morning, not some spur-of-the-moment desire. She couldn't work like this and be effective. She was about to stress the importance of pre-outing information, but the dark circles underneath Jo's eyes made her reconsider. "Ms. West, are you sure you're all right? You can go see this movie another time, you know."

"I know. But I want to go now. I need some excitement and I'm not going to get that at home. Besides, I know I have nothing to worry about because I'll have my protector with me the entire time. Right?"

Lee smiled. She couldn't help it. "Try to get rid of me."

CHAPTER EIGHT

Jo waited patiently while the theater cleared. She had enjoyed the action flick and adrenaline coursed through her veins, but her excitement had nothing to do with the movie and everything to do with the woman standing a few feet away scanning the room for potential danger.

Before the movie had started, Lee had been unusually talkative. She'd asked questions about the characters and plot and was more open than Jo had yet seen her. When the trailers began to roll, not only did the lights dim but Lee's enthusiasm seemed to have faded along with them. She wanted to believe it was because Lee had been disappointed that their conversation had come to an end, but that couldn't be right, could it? She'd be foolish to think that Lee's willingness to talk was due to anything but filling the silence that had stretched between them. Still, Jo had found her charming and surprisingly funny.

As the movie progressed, she even noticed Lee's formal nature and stiff posture begin to subside. But halfway through the movie when bombs started exploding and screams rattled the theater, the rigid posture had returned, along with the familiar tensing of her jaw. She wasn't even sure if Lee was cognizant of her nervous habit, but it pained Jo to watch her struggle. At one point, she'd motioned Lee over in an attempt to get her to sit down by her, but Lee refused. She had placed her hand on Lee's arm to get her to look at her in an effort to calm her, to soothe away whatever demons she had been fighting. The roped muscles had rippled beneath her hand but eventually quieted under her soothing caress. She had enjoyed how the tight muscles danced under her fingertips. Lee had moved away shortly afterward and never overtly acknowledged the contact, but she'd slightly quirked her lips.

They slowly made their way outside, the mass of people milling around making it hard for Jo to maneuver safely on her crutches. She braced herself against Lee a few times, more out of a desire to touch her than the need for balance. She leaned heavily on her crutches as they waited for their car beneath a brilliant sunset. Lee looked around and frowned before calling the driver, who was stuck in traffic. The temperature had cooled considerably, but not as much as Lee's attitude. She was once again aloof and annoyingly controlled.

"So, what did you think of the movie?"

"It was good."

"That's your critical analysis?" Jo laughed. "A film critic you're not."

"Apparently not."

Robot. "What did you think of Hugh Jackman? He's pretty hot, huh?"

"He's very good looking, yes."

Jo wanted to grab Lee and shake her. She hated Lee's bodyguard persona, one she took too fucking seriously. The controlled, only need-to-know, one-word answers were grating on what few nerves she had left. Once again it reminded her of the control people had over her life.

Getting information out of Lee was like picking a lock. She had to be precise with her questions and hope she asked the right ones to get Lee to open up. She did have one question she'd been wanting to ask since the small sex scene with the lead actor and his on-screen girlfriend. Lee's face had been the picture of concentration during that time, and Jo didn't think it had anything to do with the hunky Hugh Jackman. "And what about the woman who played his girlfriend?"

"Lynn Collins?"

"Ha! You were paying attention."

The corners of Lee's mouth turned up in a playful grin. "I always pay attention, especially when it matters."

"Really? And…what did you think of her?"

Lee appeared to be considering her next words carefully. "She's…*hot* too."

"That, she is." Jo smiled. Awesome. Another door expertly opened. Since she seemed to be on a roll today she opted for a little more prying. "I'm glad you enjoyed the movie. Speaking of enjoying, are you enjoying your position as a glorified babysitter? It's been a little over two weeks since you took on the guardian-angel role."

"I wouldn't call it babysitting," Lee said, removing her jacket. "And trust me, I'm no angel. Cold?"

"A little," Jo said as Lee placed the jacket around her shoulders. "Thanks. So what would you call yourself, exactly?"

"An employee," Lee said simply. "I'm like any other person. I wake up, go to work, go home."

Jo wanted to say Lee was far from someone who held a mundane job where they blended into the background like some drone working in the hive for the queen bee. But the more she thought about it, the more she understood Lee's assessment. Tory was the queen bee calling the shots, and Lee was a drone who buzzed around the house, only used when called upon. The thought saddened her. "That simple, huh?" Jo inhaled slowly, finding comfort in Lee's familiar scent of amber and spice.

"Yes."

"Do you have a family?"

"No."

"A lover?"

Lee stared at her intently. "No."

Jo swallowed hard, chancing one more question. "You seemed to have found Lynn Collins attractive. So, if you had a choice, blondes or brunettes?"

Jo couldn't see Lee's eyes behind the dark sunglasses, but the tension in her body had returned, along with the slight twitch of her jaw. The switch appeared to have been flipped. The barriers that had been briefly lowered between them had once again returned to their full and original position.

The Lincoln Town Car pulled in front of the theater, drawing a few curious stares. Lee held the door open for Jo, but she refused to get in until Lee answered her question. "Waiting."

Lee removed her dark sunglasses, holding Jo's gaze unerringly. "Blondes. Always blondes."

Lee focused her attention on the passing scenery to keep her eyes and mind occupied. Jo hadn't said a word since they'd left the theater. Swearing inwardly, she wanted to blame her restlessness on her PTSD, but that excuse was wearing thin. What ailed her had nothing to do with her medical condition.

Damn! How could one touch in a crowded theater make her reexamine all her priorities? She knew her job and did it well. But for one moment when Jo had touched her, she'd forgotten all about those priorities. Forgotten the reasons why she had been there with Jo in the first place. All she had been aware of was what had passed between them. Something she was unfamiliar with, a sense that someone could actually understand her suffering. But that was crazy. Jo couldn't understand her. She'd never been to war, never seen people blown to pieces in front of her, people she'd once called friends. There was nothing sexual in the touch, yet she couldn't help responding to it.

The more she thought about it, the more her skin tingled, rippled, with an undercurrent of arousal she hadn't experienced in a long time. As Jo's scent wafted over her, she picked up on the distinct mixture of warm sand and sea air. The familiar fragrance reminded her of a tropical beach and she imagined being stretched out on a towel on the sand, no one around except Jo, the sun coloring Jo's pale skin a warm bronze. She closed her eyes, picturing Jo lying between her legs, teasing her clit as the sounds of her cries became lost among the roaring of the ocean and the shrieks of the gulls overhead. Jo took her between those full lips and sucked—*Christ!*

Lee jumped when Jo placed a hand on her arm. This was exactly why she had to keep a professional distance. Jo was inquisitive by nature. She liked to touch and tried at every opportunity to worm her way into Lee's orderly life. She couldn't chance feeling anything more for Jo, especially since that touch from her earlier had her all stirred up.

"Hey, everything okay?" Jo asked as the car pulled up in front of the house.

"Everything's fine, Ms. West. Hold on. Let me go around to your side." Lee walked around to open Jo's door just as Tory jogged down the steps to meet them.

"Hey, honey," Tory said as Lee assisted her out of the car. She kissed Jo's cheek. "How you holding up?"

"If it wasn't for my bodyguard, I don't think I'd be holding anything up," Jo said as Lee grasped her waist until she adjusted the crutches safely under her arms.

"Do you need my help getting upstairs?" Tory asked.

"No, I'm okay. Just tired. Call me when dinner's ready."

"You bet."

Jo disappeared into the house and Tory motioned for Lee to follow her into the office. Lee sat to the left of Tory's manager, who didn't look pleased.

"Lee, I asked you here because the group and I have finally decided to tour this summer," Tory said. "I think you're perfect for Jo and she appears to like you. I wanted to know if you'd be interested in traveling with us? I'm sure Jo will argue about accompanying the group, but I was hoping to plead my case with your help. What do you say? I could really use her there for backup."

What do I say? I say you're out of your mind, lady! She's just been in a horrible accident and needs a nap after a few hours out. Didn't you just see her? Six months on the road will kill her. "Ma'am, I don't mind the work if she still wants me around." *Which I highly doubt after she recovers fully.* "But I don't think it's a good idea for me to encourage her in any way. It's not my job to convince her to travel, just to make sure she's safe."

"My sister values your opinion, Lee, whether you believe that or not. I can tell. She trusts you and I want to make sure she stays safe. It goes without saying that she'll want to stay here, but I feel that if I can persuade her to leave the country with us for a while, this business of the stalker will eventually fade and ultimately disappear. We'll leave the situation behind us, and I'll know Jo's safe because she'll be there with me. And of course, she'll step in like she always does when I overbook." Tory smiled, clearly convinced she was right.

Lee placed her hands into her trouser pockets to hide their trembling. Just mentioning the stalker and Jo in the same sentence made her want to run from the room and find Jo to make sure she was all right. This problem wasn't going away, and Tory was a fool if she actually believed what she was saying. "Ms. West—"

"Tory."

Lee conceded. "Ma'am, may I be blunt?"

"I expect nothing else from you, Lee."

"I'm worried about your decision. Your sister is still not a hundred percent, and even if she agrees to travel, her physical condition will make it more difficult for me to protect her when she's out in the open. She's stubborn and refuses all help even when I offer."

At this comment Tory didn't even try to hide a smile. "Anything else?"

"Yes. As you know, I'm no expert, but if you leave before dealing with this potentially dangerous situation, you will only exacerbate the problem."

Marilyn butted in. "Then what do you propose we do? This is wearing Tory down, and God only knows what being holed up for a lengthy period of time will do to Jo. They can't hide here forever. The band needs to tour."

That's easy to answer if you'd both just take a second to look at her. Since Lee spent a lot of time studying Jo, she couldn't ignore the shadows beneath Jo's eyes that suggested she wasn't sleeping. The pain medication obviously made her groggy and irritable. She barely ate. She wasn't ready for anything strenuous. "My suggestion *again* would be to bring in the proper authorities to help find this lunatic before he acts out and hurts someone else. He's already proved that he can be violent, and we don't know what he has in store for another surprise. If you bring her out into the open before Gary has a chance to figure out his next move, she or someone else you know may get hurt."

Tory sat stone-faced, obviously weighing the options. She leaned forward, her look of concentration turning to one of fierce determination. "I appreciate your candor, but we will proceed with the tour schedule as planned. I won't have this maniac run our lives, and I don't want the kind of press it would bring if we contacted the police. If you'd like to join us on the road we'll be glad to have you. If not, I'll make other arrangements for Jo's security. Because I'm sure she'll be with us."

Over my dead body. Jo was her responsibility, and unless Jo personally dismissed her, Lee wasn't going anywhere. Lee stood and looked down at Tory. "I'll let you know my decision pending your sister's choice."

CHAPTER NINE

L ee returned from her morning run just as the predawn light poured bright streaks between the grayish clouds that marred the early morning sky. She felt strong, exhilarated. Shaking the rainwater and sweat out of her hair, she grabbed a towel and straddled her weight bench, intent on pushing her muscles to the limit. The weeks of working out regularly had started to pay off. What had begun as three miles a day with an hour of intense martial arts training had turned into an additional two miles a day plus an added hour of every other day upper and lower body lifting.

Since their visit to the theater a few weeks ago, Jo had become more mobile by the day, and it wouldn't be much longer before she'd be able to move around without needing crutches. The scars on her face had healed nicely and the bruising had long since faded. Lee had hoped the stalker situation would have been resolved before Jo fully healed. They hadn't received any more letters, though, or any reports of anyone unusual hanging around the house. Without more to go on, Gary and his friends were at a loss. She worried about what would happen once Jo decided she was strong enough to move out of her sister's life. She most likely wouldn't keep a bodyguard once she was out of Tory's limelight.

She switched on the television, not paying much attention to the activity buzzing on the screen that marked the beginning of some type of press conference. She cranked up the volume and finished her last set of chest presses, leaving her only a half hour to eat breakfast and shower before returning to Jo's. Moving into the kitchen, she quickly filled a blender with a banana, yogurt, protein powder, and ice. As she strained to hear the television over the sounds of crushed ice, she caught only snippets of the conversation regarding some kind of upcoming concert tour. Pouring her breakfast into a glass, she raised her head as a familiar name caught her attention. She leaned over the counter and stretched as far as her six-foot frame would allow, swiveling the television to face her. *What the fuck?*

Looking composed and confident, Tory West stood at a wooden podium in full costume and makeup, surrounded by three of the other band members. "Ladies and gentlemen," Tory said. "The group and I are here today to publicly announce Total Femme's international tour schedule. Our Leather and Lace Tour will cover six countries in twenty-four weeks. I'll answer a few questions then turn the mic over to the other group members."

"Oh, shit." Lee had no idea a press conference was happening today and only hoped that Tory had been adequately prepared for any questions those blood-sucking reporters had in mind. Lord knows, they very rarely stayed on topic, and thankfully, from the looks of things, Jo didn't seem to be there.

"First question?" Tory said as the crowd yelled out her name. She pointed to a fifty-something reporter with a bad hairpiece and thinning mustache. "Go ahead."

"Yes…thank you. I'm James Mayfield with the *Tribune*," he said as the crowd quieted. "I was wondering if you'd give us a bit of insight into the man who has been sending you threatening letters. Do you or the police have any leads?"

Tory showed no signs of being rattled, but Lee felt like she'd been hit in the stomach with a lead pipe.

"Mr. Mayfield, I can't answer your question because I have no idea what you're talking about. Next question, please?"

Mayfield snickered at Tory's attempt to downplay the situation, and a low murmur could be heard among the other reporters.

"That's not what I heard. In fact, a very reliable source told me this person has sent you dozens of letters. They also suggested that it wasn't you in the limo the night of the car crash but your twin sister pretending to be you. Is that true and was she the intended target?"

"No, no, no!" Lee shouted at the television. This is exactly what she'd feared. "Come on, Tory. Keep cool." Lee stood in front of the TV, trying hard not to punch something.

"Mr. Mayfield, I seriously doubt you know more than the police do. I made a statement after the accident from the hospital and I'm sticking to it. Now if anyone has any relevant questions regarding the tour, I will be happy to answer those at this time. Otherwise, I'll hand the mic over to our bass player, Chance Dillingham."

The crowd buzzed with excitement, and the words "stalker" and "conspiracy" were being thrown out at regular intervals. The media sharks smelled blood and were circling. In their frenzy they waited until they spotted a vulnerable spot to attack.

"Fuck," Lee growled, knowing that whoever this Mayfield prick was, he'd just made her job ten times harder. "I'm gonna kill that asshole." She grabbed her jacket and ran out the door, pressing one on her phone for speed dial.

"Lee, what took you so long?" Gary said. "I expected your call about ten seconds earlier."

"What the *hell*, Gary? How come I wasn't told about a press conference, and how did this bastard get that information?" Lee jumped on her Yamaha, firing up the powerful engine.

"I didn't know about it until about ten minutes before it happened. I knew the girls were rehearsing this morning, but the press conference was a last-minute idea by Tory. As for the other issue, I'm damn well gonna find out."

"You better. I'm headed over to the West home now. Keep me apprised of whatever intel you get in the next few hours. I want everything you have on this jerk-off reporter, from what he eats for breakfast to his underwear size. As soon as I know Jo's safe, I'll call you back for an update."

"Roger that."

Lee peeled out of the parking lot, setting a speed record by arriving at the West home in five minutes flat. She ran up the front steps, nearly crashing into a hulk of a man as he pulled the door open.

"Staff Sergeant Winters," he said, extending his large hand. "Corporal Simons."

Who? Now what the fuck have you done, Tory? Lee took one step back, appraising the man who stood before her who had done everything but salute. "Simons, when were you hired?"

"This morning. I arrived at 0500."

Damn it! The whole day was turning into a cluster fuck. "And what were your orders?"

"That I was to remain here to keep an eye on Jolene West until you returned."

This was just fucking fantastic. Tory most likely got this Simons name from one of Gary's list of available pre-screened bodyguards but didn't tell Gary that she would be contacting him directly. To make matters worse, Tory had left this man in charge of Jo, without telling *her*. She immediately took stock of him. Six-six, two-fifty, give or take a few pounds, traditional military flat top. After the press conference and the Mayfield incident, she'd rip Gary a new one if he knew anything about this and didn't notify her before arriving. Jo was her responsibility. She made the decisions regarding her protection. Not Tory. Not Gary.

It also didn't go unnoticed that this new bodyguard had called her by her former title. A lot of information holes needed to be plugged today. If she found the source of the leakage, she'd make sure they thought twice about ever revealing confidences again. Simons wasn't at fault. He'd only used the term out of respect, but Lee wasn't feeling diplomatic after the morning's events. "Simons, I am no longer employed by the United States military. If you wish to call me Lee or ma'am, that's fine, but under no circumstances are you allowed to call me by my former rank. Do I make myself clear?"

"Yes, ma'am," he said, nearly standing at attention.

Lee glanced past Simons, noticing a contingent of maids and butlers. She'd received a list of Tory's planned engagements from Gary just yesterday but couldn't recall seeing anything listed for today. A large banquet table was being set with flowers and fine china, and the kitchen staff had to have tripled in size. "Simons, what's going on?"

"I'm sorry?"

"What are all these people doing here, Simons? I wasn't aware of a party this evening." *Jesus, this fucking day just keeps getting better and better.*

"Oh, sorry. I almost forgot." He reached into his coat pocket and handed her a guest list. "Ms. West told me to give you this."

Lee unfolded the sheet of paper, her anger tripling as she read the guest list for the surprise tour-launch party. Simons was there to keep an eye on the caterers until Tory returned from the studio. "God damn it!" Lee pressed her fingers to her temple to stop the headache forming behind her eyes. "How many people knew about this?"

"Not sure, ma'am." He shrugged. "But according to Dan Powers, Tory West's primary bodyguard, it's not unusual for Ms. West to do things last minute."

Unfortunately, Lee was becoming quickly schooled in this adverse fact. "Fanfuckintastic!" She pinched the bridge of her nose and took a deep breath. "Where is Jolene West now?"

"I assume she's still asleep in her room. Haven't seen her since I arrived."

"You assume?" Lee glared at the ex-soldier as he took one step back. She'd had enough of incompetence for one day. "You assume! Didn't anyone ever tell you in the service that assumptions are the mother of all fuck-ups?"

"I…yes…"

"Have. You. Seen. Her?"

"No, ma'am."

Lee angrily pushed past him, taking the stairs two at a time. When she arrived at Jo's door, it took all her control not to burst into the room. She knocked but received no answer. "Ms. West, may I speak with you?" She pushed the door open to peek through the crack she created. "Ms. West?"

At first glance, Lee didn't notice anything out of place. There were no signs of a struggle. Clothes were neatly folded on the rumpled bed. A half-eaten bagel sat on a plate by the bed next to an empty bottle of water. *Damn it, where is she?*

Lee listened for a moment but still didn't hear anything. She glanced at the bathroom and wondered if Jo had fallen and knocked herself out or something. She decided to check, but before she could move, Jo opened the bathroom door and emerged totally naked from the shower, dripping from head to toe with steam rising off her flushed skin. The smell of plumeria and coconut quickly assaulted Lee's senses.

Jo moved across the room and was within inches of the bed before she screamed and jumped back, losing her grip on the crutches and crashing onto the bed below.

Lee's feet had to have been glued to the floor because why else couldn't she move? She was glad Jo had fallen onto the bed, because even if she could have reacted, reaching for a naked Jolene West would have been a problem on so many levels.

"What the hell?" Jo quickly yanked a bed sheet over her body. "What are you doing in here?"

"I'm sorry," Lee said, backing away slowly. "I knocked… but…you didn't answer, and I thought…" Lee grasped blindly for the door behind her. It had to be there somewhere. She swallowed hard as Jo rose, wrapping the bed sheet around herself.

"You thought?" Jo asked, moving closer while balancing expertly on one crutch.

"I'm sorry," Lee said, regaining her composure. "I shouldn't have barged in. Please accept my apology. I should go."

"Hold on." Jo grabbed Lee's forearm to stop her. "Stay. You obviously have a reason for being here. Can it wait until I get dressed?"

Lee nodded but kept her eyes focused on the far wall. She couldn't look at the soft hand resting on her bare skin. It would undo her. "Of course. I'll be right outside. Call me when you're ready."

"Nonsense. Sit." Jo pushed Lee into the chair next to her bed. "This will only take a second."

Lee wished she had the strength to look somewhere, anywhere, other than at Jo's half-naked body as she moved into the walk-in closet to gather some clothes. Jo had an unbelievable figure—tight, round breasts and a subtle curve to her hips, even visible through the thin sheet. And just when she thought she'd regained all her composure, Jo dropped the sheet at the entrance to the closet, making Lee realize that no matter how honorable she was, nothing could make her take her eyes off the beautiful sight before her. *Oh shit! Don't react. Keep your cool, soldier.*

"Okay, you were saying," Jo said, stepping into a pair of boxers and tank top. Lee swallowed hard, unable to concentrate on anything but the form-fitting boxers and skimpy tank that outlined every one of those luscious curves.

Jesus, I'm not going to survive this!

"Like what you see?" Jo asked, clearly amused with Lee's loss for words.

Lee nodded. It was all she could do.

"I'll take that as a yes." Jo grinned. "If you can't answer that question, how about telling me why you're here early?"

"I'm here…" Lee said hoarsely, clearing her throat. Thank God she was sitting down. "As I was saying, your sister held a press conference today regarding Total Femme's upcoming international tour."

"What press conference?"

Lee sighed. "Believe me, it was as much of a surprise to me as to you. I'm sure your sister will update you when she returns, but with all the events she has planned, you're going to need another bodyguard—"

"No."

"Pardon?"

"You heard me," Jo said. "How much clearer do I need to be?"

"But, Ms. West, with the number of people invited to the party this evening—"

"Wait a minute. Party? What the hell! Here…tonight?"

Lee rubbed her eyes in frustration. Her job wasn't to announce Tory West's engagements. She resented the star for putting her in this position and for the first time understood how Jo must feel living with someone with Tory's devil-may-give-a-shit attitude. No wonder Jo wanted to get away from all this. "When I arrived this morning, the staff was setting up for a tour-launch party. Yes, here. Tonight. I was told that most of the other members of the group would be present."

"Where's Tory? I need to talk with her. This is bullshit!"

"I have no idea." Lee stood, happy to have regained some control. She was glad she wasn't the only one irritated. "I need to discuss some details with Gary, but before I go, do you have any plans for today?"

"Nothing except maybe read my new book. Shit! Now I need to have yet another conversation with my sister, who still hasn't learned she can't make these kinds of decisions in this house without discussing them with me first."

Ha! Welcome to my world. Now maybe you'll understand that guarding you has been no picnic. "Just notify me if you decide to leave the house and I'll be waiting."

Jo grumbled something unintelligible as Lee left the room and dialed Gary's number. She didn't like surprises, no soldier did. Often they got people killed, and unfortunately, if Tory kept this up, they all might very well get an unwanted surprise that could eventually cost someone their life.

Lee sat in the small lobby of the San Francisco branch of Diamond Records waiting for Tory to arrive. She'd been summoned an hour ago and didn't have to wait long for the clearly upset Total Femme star to enter, followed by Marilyn, Dan, and a small, balding man who looked like he'd pull his hair out if he had some to spare. Tory loomed over the man's desk, yelling obscenities as he swiveled absently in his chair.

"What the hell, Larry?" Tory yelled, slamming her wig down on his desk. "I was supposed to answer a few harmless questions about touring. How did this creep get information about my mysterious letter writer? No one knows except the few people in this room and a couple of the bodyguards."

"Tory, calm down," Larry said, putting his hands up as if to avoid an assault. "Give me a second to think. And who the hell are you?" he asked, pointing to Lee.

Tory turned to Lee. "Hey, Lee, glad you could make it."

"No problem, ma'am. But like I stated on the phone, I need to return to the house within the hour to accompany your sister on an outing."

"Let's make this quick then." She introduced Lee to Larry Newman, Total Femme's chief publicist. "Did you see the press conference?"

"Yes," Lee said.

"Then you realize that we currently have a publicity nightmare on our hands. The phone hasn't stopped ringing with requests for interviews—about Jo being injured, about the stalker. About... everything," Larry said. Sweat stains at the armpits marred his expensive shirt, and he continually fiddled with a pen.

Lee didn't know exactly how much Tory had told Larry about the situation, so her only indication that she'd heard him was a slight quirk of her eyebrow. She didn't care for his unprofessional outbursts or his tone.

"Lee, you can relax," Tory said. "Larry knows everything."

Lee studied Tory in surprise. No doubt loving a soldier had given her an advantage over others when it came to reading one, because she looked away quickly. "If he knows everything," Lee said, turning her attention back to Larry, "then he must also realize that you have more than just a publicity nightmare on your hands."

"What is she talking about?" Tory shot a hard look in Larry's direction.

"Tory," he said in exasperation, "I explained to you earlier that I didn't think this press conference was a good idea, remember?"

"Yeah, so? And I believe I told *you* that I pay you a lot of money to stop thinking about what's best for my personal life and worry about my public one. The girls and I agreed that we had to announce this tour. You're the one always telling me that publicity is good whether it's positive or negative."

"When am I ever going to get you to realize that you no longer have a private life? In fact, I believe you told me you had this argument with your sister a few days ago."

"Leave Jo out of this and just tell me!"

"Ma'am, if I could explain?" Lee said, getting Tory to look at her. "You have just denied the stalker's love for you on national television by telling the world he doesn't exist. According to Gary's source, someone with his personality won't take that denial lightly."

"Which means?"

"His delusions revolve around the idea that he's in love with you and that you love him back. Denying his love alters his delusion, making him feel rejected and abandoned. He's likely to lash out at the first opportunity."

Tory paled and swayed. "Oh, my God." Tory swayed, and Lee gripped her arm to steady her. "Where's Jo? Someone call her. Make sure she's okay—"

"Don't worry. She's in good hands. Gary and I will do everything we can to protect you and your sister." Lee helped Tory into a chair. "But you need to understand that surprises like today are not going to help your situation. We always need to be aware of everything you're planning so we can be prepared for these sort of instances when they occur."

"Gary? Who the hell is this Gary?" Larry asked like the name left a bad taste in his mouth.

"Look..." Lee said. "One more word—"

"Lee," Tory said, "I got this. Larry, you don't need to know who he is. Just know he will do everything he can to help us clear up this mess without involving the authorities."

"Not involve the authorities?" Larry asked, seeming incredulous. "Tory, you don't have much of a choice after today. In fact, I can't believe the cops aren't breaking down my door after all this talk of a supposed stalker."

"Neither can I, but that's where you come in. Concentrate on the positives of the tour, and if anyone asks anything else about this subject say, 'No comment.' Advertise the tour, get in touch with the promoters, and keep Marilyn apprised of anything I need to know about, but I mean it, Larry...no one...I mean no one, is to mention this again. Got it? I'm sick of it."

Larry slammed his glasses on the table and rubbed his eyes. "You're the boss. But if we don't find who leaked this information, I don't know how effective I can be at damage control."

"Don't worry about that," Lee said, rising with Tory. "Leave it up to me."

CHAPTER TEN

The man screamed in rage while frantically assembling another letter. Tory had denied her love for him to the entire world, and for that it would cost her something extra. He would teach her a lesson and she'd realize her mistake. She'd looked so beautiful, so perfect in every way, until she opened her mouth and lied about them, about their love.

"What are you doing?" the Angry Man asked.

"Why do you care?"

"I care because you're an idiot and whatever you have planned will never work."

The man stared defiantly at his tormentor. "Of course it will *work*. You'll see," he said, sealing the envelope.

"I thought you were planning to meet her? Show her how charming you are."

"I was, but plans change. She changed things. She has to see."

The Angry Man laughed hysterically. "You finally realize she'll never come around. Am I right?"

The man bowed his head and whispered, "She will... eventually."

"So why the new letter?"

"It's a secret," the man said, placing his finger to his lips.

"What secret! You tell me everything."

The man returned his attention to the precious envelope, rotating the paper back and forth in front of his face. The excitement built between his legs, but he would save himself for Tory because nothing else could compare. "And look where it's gotten me."

He glanced down at the picture of Tory on the front page of the *Times*, ignoring the taunts in the background. "This time, my love, your denial means someone has to die. Then it'll be me you turn to for comfort, and the world will know the truth. You're mine."

CHAPTER ELEVEN

Jo walked out of the dressing room and took stock of her appearance in the full-length mirror. Lee leaned against the wall in the empty hallway, one hand in her pocket and the other checking her BlackBerry. She hoped Lee would offer an opinion on the color and style of the dress she'd chosen for the evening and was about to ask when Lee looked up and pushed away from the wall, an expression of awe on her handsome face.

"You look beautiful."

"Really?" Jo asked, self-consciously smoothing an imaginary wrinkle out of the satin material. "You don't think it's too much? I know with the cast and crutches I probably look ridiculous but..."

Lee continued to stare at her. "This really isn't my expertise, Ms. West."

Jo held her crutches tightly and looked away. How stupid of her to think Lee would offer an opinion. Lee was an employee, a hired hand. But what she'd seen in Lee's eyes a few seconds ago had given her hope that, for once, Lee would look at her as more than a job. Obviously, she'd been wrong. The rebuff hurt. "Never mind. Forget I asked." She turned to limp back to the dressing room.

"But," Lee whispered, as if Jo hadn't spoken, "I think it's perfect."

Jo looked over her shoulder and glanced into the liquid, dark eyes. Her heart thundered. No feeling in the world could match having Lee gaze at her that way. "Thanks," she said as Lee slowly backed away. "Let me change and I'll take you to lunch. Be right out."

She returned moments later to find Lee pacing outside her dressing-room door. Something in Lee's serious expression told her Lee was plotting another one of her lame "we shouldn't" excuses. She'd used the excuse numerous times since she had barged into her bedroom and seen her naked. This time, though, Jo was prepared. She closed the gap between them, stopping Lee's pacing with a hand on her chest.

Jo watched the churn of emotions play across Lee's face. Curiosity. Fear. Desire. She hadn't meant to touch her, but she didn't want to hear any more excuses as to why they couldn't have something as simple as lunch together. Lee's muscles tensed beneath her fingertips. Her heartbeat thudded violently against Jo's palm. She stepped back but Jo followed, her eyes transfixed on the pulse pounding wildly in Lee's neck. Jo wanted to place her mouth there, suck on that vital lifeline until Lee succumbed to the pleasure. As she slowly pulled her hand away, she was surprised when Lee swayed slightly toward her as if the connection couldn't be broken. "Just in case you planned on declining my lunch offer," Jo said a little breathlessly, "forget it, because it's not negotiable. I'm hungry and you need to eat."

Lee glanced down at Jo's hand before returning her steady gaze. "As you wish."

The irony in that statement made Jo laugh. If Lee knew her wishes, neither one of them would leave the dressing room anytime soon. As she pushed past Lee, she could feel the warm gaze on her back. The heat seared her skin and left her feeling invigorated and very much alive.

Lunch at the popular Chinese restaurant was in full swing as Lee sat across from Jo at the two-person table near the closest exit, her back to the wall, her eyes glued to the front entrance. She couldn't relax for many reasons, the main one being that she shouldn't be socializing with Jo while she was being paid to protect her.

She should have been able to find a way to subtly decline lunch, but the wounded look in Jo's eyes had made her reconsider. Denying her attraction to Jo at this point was futile. But what she felt recently had far surpassed attraction and turned into something even more dangerous. Attachment was something she hadn't counted on—needing to be near Jo all the time, worrying about her when they were apart. These were the things she'd never considered feeling for anyone. In the service, orders were carried out and emotions were left behind. She'd never had to worry about anyone but herself and the men who reported to her.

Growing up in foster homes with no family to speak of meant she'd always been alone. But as every barrier dropped between them, she worried she'd make a mistake. In war, mistakes got a person killed. And she *was* at war—with a stalker, a faceless threat she couldn't assess properly. Eventually she'd beat him at his own game, and she wouldn't stop short of killing him if he even batted an eyelash in Jo's direction. But she was also waging a war with her heart. She'd never been afraid of anything in her life, but if she was going to be honest with herself, these feelings for Jo had no place in her orderly life and were scaring the shit out of her.

"Lee, you need to relax," Jo said, placing her menu on the table. "I doubt there's anyone here that wants to do me harm."

"You don't know that, Ms. West." She scanned the restaurant once more, making sure nothing seemed out of the ordinary. Given their position inside the restaurant and her vantage point for trouble, they were as safe as they could be, given the situation.

"Okay, look. Please try to relax a little. We're having lunch. I want us to have a nice time and not have it feel like an interrogation. We've been spending a lot of time together lately and I want us to become acquainted. I know *friends* get in the way of your priorities. And even though I don't like the idea that I'm a responsibility to you, we can at least get to know one another a little better. So, no more *Ms. West* nonsense. I'm ordering you to call me Jo. And don't you military types have to follow orders by the people who are in charge?"

Interesting way of looking at it. "Okay, Jo…is that better?"

"Much." Jo's smile was infectious and Lee couldn't help but smile along with her. "Now are you going to pick something, or do I have to order for the both of us?" Jo asked.

"Not really hungry, so whatever you'd like to order is fine."

"Really?" Jo leaned forward onto her elbows. "And what if my tastes aren't to your liking?"

Unable to resist the clear double entendre, Lee leaned close, locking her eyes on Jo's lips. "I'm sure your *tastes* will satisfy my appetite just fine."

The blush that stole up Jo's cheeks painted her face with a healthy glow. Quickly, she retreated behind her menu. "That's good to know because I'm starving."

Holy shit! Flirting! Talk about being out of control. What the hell was she thinking? She would've fired someone on the spot for the inappropriate behavior. Without her self-control she'd have nothing left. She scanned the room again.

They ordered and sat for the next few minutes in awkward silence. Not talking was bordering on rude, so Lee decided to take control of the questions and break the tension between them. "Did you always live in this area?"

"Yeah. Not too far from here actually. My parents owned a small home on the outskirts of Redwood City."

"You sound fond of it."

"How can you tell?"

"Your voice, the tone you used. Melancholy, I guess. Like you miss it."

"You're very perceptive," Jo said, but there was no malice behind her words.

"One of my annoying traits, I believe you said." Lee smiled.

"It can be at times, but this isn't one of them."

"So tell me about this home." Lee tried to ignore Jo's melodious, flirty tone that caused a pool of wetness to form between her legs. Her body had a mind of its own where Jo was concerned.

"It was cute, small, but we managed. The house was close to Cordilleras Creek. Tory and I used to play near the creek all the time. We built a playhouse in the back…Well, my dad did." Jo's eyes became distant, sad, the memory obviously painful to relive. "How about you? Have family near here?"

You opened yourself up to this line of questioning. Deal with it. "I grew up in foster homes."

"And after that?"

"When I was eighteen I joined the service. The people I served with were my family."

"Were?"

"I'm sorry?"

"You said 'were.' Do you keep in touch with anyone besides Gary?"

Lee took a deep breath. "No. "

"Why?"

Lee lowered her head and pushed the appetizers in front of her around on her plate. The permanent stake in her heart was being painfully twisted, and she tried to swallow around the lump in her throat. "Because they're all dead."

Lee couldn't bear to look into Jo's eyes. Something told her she'd see sympathy there, maybe even pity. She didn't deserve it for something that was all her fault. Their lives had been her responsibility and she had failed them. All of them. She would have gladly given up her life if they could have all lived. But she'd let them down and now she lived her days and nights in hell. She closed her eyes in an effort to focus, and suddenly she was thrust back to Ramadi. She could smell fire, death.

She searched the building, trying to clear the smoke and dust from her eyes. Soldiers were screaming all around her, but what

*scared her most was the eerie silence that followed once those
cries died away. She'd managed to carry a few soldiers from the
burning building, returning for a final sweep when she noticed
Corporal Lance Fiero, lying in a pool of blood. His legs had been
blown from his body, the vacant look of death staring at her from
dead eyes. She could never leave a soldier behind. As she dragged
him out of the building she heard another soldier scream in the
darkness and dust, and vowed to return for him when the building
exploded for the second time that day. The world flew past her in
shredded hunks of debris before everything went black.*

"Hey," Jo said as Lee opened her eyes. "You okay?"

Lee glanced blankly at Jo, momentarily forgetting where she
was. She looked around the crowded restaurant. Bodies weren't
scattered around her. The smell of death was absent. Another
flashback. Damn. "I'm fine."

"Oh, Lee," Jo said, covering Lee's hand with her own. "I'm
sorry if my question brought up bad memories."

"Please, don't be. It's my cross to bear. Not yours."

"Would you like to talk about it?"

A slight tremor ran through Lee and sweat dripped down her
back, even though the room was cool. "I…"

"Hey," Jo said, tugging on Lee's hand to get her to look at
her. "I want to hear this but how about another time? When you're
ready. Okay?"

"Thanks." Lee offered Jo a half smile, not knowing if she'd
ever be ready for that kind of confession.

Food arrived at a steady pace as their conversation moved
on to more mundane topics. They ate and talked, and although
Lee continued to keep an eye on their surroundings, she relaxed
enough to enjoy their meal and the sound of Jo's voice.

"I noticed you like to read," Lee said. "Any particular genre?"

"Romance," Jo said around a bite of moo shoo pork.

"Ah…where the guy rides in on his white horse and whisks
the girl away."

"Close. I'm actually hoping that one day a woman will whisk me away."

"Ah…I see."

"So why the question?"

"Knowledge, really," Lee said around another bite. "The more I know about you from you, no matter how minute the detail, the safer you'll be. Good intel is everything."

"I see," Jo said, disappointed. She'd hoped Lee's questions were because she really wanted to know, not because of work. Ever since Jo was little, Tory had always garnered the most attention. She was always the smarter twin—the more talented twin. Jo had always come second to Tory because she never asked for anything except to be her own person. After Tory had become famous, it was worse. She'd been sucked into being an underling for Tory's career and had lost her freedom in the process.

For the most part, Jo tried not to let any of that get to her. But when it came to Lee's attention, she wanted to be her sole focus. To find out that their lunch had moved into the business-as-usual category, especially after Lee's confession earlier, saddened her. She refused to cry and tried desperately to blink away stubborn tears of frustration. Suddenly Lee pushed away from the table and knelt in front of her on one knee.

"Hey, what's wrong? Not feeling well?"

Could this get any more embarrassing? Not only was Lee kneeling in front of her in a crowded restaurant, but she had caught her in a moment of self-pity. All her life she'd wanted to be seen as her own person, and with Lee it had become even more important to be regarded as more than a job. As the familiar feelings resurfaced, she bit back the angry retort, knowing she couldn't be mad at Lee for something that wasn't her fault. "I'm okay. Guess I'm just tired."

Lee wiped away a stray tear with her thumb. "Well, it has been a long day."

"Yeah, it has. Sorry. I'm not normally like this."

"No need to be sorry. What do you say we finish lunch and then go home so you can rest before the party. Deal?"

Jo looked down into the unguarded eyes, amazed at Lee's sudden transformation. How could someone be so distant one minute and so transparent the next? The emotional teeter-tottering had Jo's head spinning. "Deal."

They finished their lunch unhurriedly, spending the next hour chatting about music and the weather. The conversation was pleasant and easy, and just as Jo was about to ask Lee about her duties in the service, Lee dropped her coffee cup onto the table, her face contorted. Jo grabbed Lee's hand, refusing to let it go when Lee tried to pull it away. She spotted the angry red scar that ended at the back of Lee's wrist and disappeared up into her sleeve.

"Sorry. My arm." Lee gritted her teeth.

"I know." Jo held Lee's hand tight, watching the unusual churn of emotions on Lee's face. Pain. Recognition. Fear. "It's okay," she said softly, tracing the scar with her fingertip. "May I?"

Lee nodded as Jo unbuttoned the cuff and rolled the shirtsleeve up past her elbow. The thick tissue ran in a snake-like pattern, disappearing behind her bicep. "I guess this is what kept you from being a Ranger?"

"Yes."

"Does it hurt?"

"Not so much anymore. Just spasms occasionally. Sorry." Lee pulled her sleeve down and abruptly pushed away from the table. "We should go. Thanks for lunch."

Lee stood as a loud crash somewhere close by caused her to swing back around and place herself protectively in front of Jo. The tension in Lee's body made Jo see why Gary had suggested her for the job. If the situation had been dangerous, Lee wouldn't have hesitated to give her life for her, a thought that instantly made Jo want to expel her lunch.

"Hey, I'm okay. Someone dropped some dishes. Relax." Jo looked around the hushed room, picking up on a few quiet murmurs. She scanned the faces of those around her who were eyeing her with curiosity. "Uh, oh," she whispered into Lee's ear. "They think I'm Tory. We're about to get bombarded."

"Ms. West!"

"Tory!"

"Can we have your autograph?"

Jo tried explaining to the crowd that quickly gathered around that she wasn't Tory West but, when that failed, told everyone she was doing well and that the scars were healing nicely. Someone even asked her about the press conference earlier and wondered how she could hide the scarring so well. Jo expertly gave Tory's makeup artist all the credit and began signing autographs until Lee started turning people away.

"This situation is getting out of hand," Lee whispered into Jo's ear before helping her to her feet.

Jo wanted to agree but for different reasons. As Lee wrapped her arm around Jo's shoulders to guide her out of the restaurant, for the second time that day she felt comforted rather than annoyed by Lee's attention. "I think you're right. How do we get out of here?"

"Leave that to me."

❖

Lee absently stared out the window at the passing scenery and regretted answering questions about her time served. She shouldn't have gone to lunch with Jo, never gotten personal. How would she ever explain to Jo why she'd survived and her men didn't? What would Jo think if she told her what had happened? That she should have been the one to die that day in Ramadi. That she gave the order that inevitably killed her men. That she lived with the devouring pain of that loss every waking moment, and most of her sleeping moments, too.

If that wasn't bad enough, Jo had seen her vulnerable, which was the last trait she would want in a bodyguard. Soldiers didn't admit weakness. Weaknesses got you killed and gave the enemy the advantage. Finally, Jo had a good excuse to fire her. No way would Lee keep her employment once Tory found out about her arm. They'd asked for the best and she'd lied. There was always a first time for everything.

Jo had asked her about the injury, but she didn't want to tell her it hurt all the time, that she constantly woke up in the middle of the night screaming in pain, and that the incessant burning was due to nerve damage that wasn't likely to heal. And tell her about the PTSD? Forget it. That would surely get her dismissed on the spot.

How amazing that a few weeks ago she didn't even want the job and now she was afraid of losing it. Maybe she should resign, save herself the humiliation of being fired and the look of disgust on Jo's face when she did it.

The car pulled up the long driveway and stopped near the steps. As usual, Tory walked down to greet them, but this time Lee could tell something was off.

"What's wrong?" Jo asked immediately.

"Nothing, sweetie. I just need to talk with Lee before the party tonight," Tory said. "Give us a minute, won't you?"

"No." Jo placed her hands defiantly on her hips. "What can't you say in front of me? And since when do we have secrets between us?"

"Ms. West," Lee said calmly, turning to face Jo. "I need to discuss the guest list with your sister at this time. Of course, you're welcome to join us if you wish."

"Why do you need to discuss that?"

"It's my job."

"Oh, yeah. That." Jo sounded irritated. "Fine, whatever. See you both tonight."

"Thank you, Lee," Tory said when Jo disappeared into the house.

"Don't thank me, ma'am. I just didn't want to stress her out more than she already is."

"That's one of the reasons I like you, Lee. You're not like the other bodyguards. You understand her. I take it she saw the press conference."

"Actually, no, but she's aware it occurred." Lee glanced at the house. Every time the stalker was mentioned, she couldn't help but search out Jo. "We discussed most of it but she refuses any additional protection."

"Big surprise," Tory said. "I'm hoping after tonight the media will focus on the upcoming tour instead of Mayfield's speculation. I have Marilyn and Larry running interference in case the tabloids start running conspiracy stories. We've threatened to sue anyone who uses the stalker story to their advantage, so that should buy us some time. I still think leaving the country will be a good thing for all of us."

Tory disappeared into the house and Lee unclipped her cell phone to call Gary. The stalker issue wasn't going away, and until Tory accepted that fact, Lee would have to be diligent in making sure every detail was covered.

"Yeah?" Gary said.

"What did you find?"

"Nothing yet. Mayfield's clean. Bastard doesn't even have a parking ticket."

"Bullshit. This guy is dirty. How about acquaintances? Family? Someone has to know something. Whoever's feeding this prick information could be the same person leaking information to our UNSUB, knowingly or unknowingly. Either way, time is running out."

"Wait!" Gary said. "I think I found something."

"What?" Lee said.

"Shit! I can't believe I missed this."

"Damn it, Gary! What the fuck is it?"

"Guess who's related to Mayfield and on Tory's payroll?"

"Do I sound like I want to play twenty fucking questions?"

"Amanda Franklin," he said, barely getting her name out before Lee slammed the phone shut and raced up the stairs.

Amanda was leaning against the kitchen wall chatting with Dan Powers when Lee grabbed the woman by the lapels and slammed her solidly into the wall.

"Lee, what the hell?" Dan shouted.

"Back off, Dan." Lee shook the woman. "Have something to say, Franklin?"

"I don't know what you're talking about." Amanda squirmed as the hands near her throat tightened.

"You might want to rethink that answer before I snap your neck." Lee tightened her grip, thinking about the trouble Amanda had already caused. If Jo got hurt…

"Wait," Amanda said, turning crimson.

Lee loosened her hold when Amanda placed her palms forward in an effort to prove she was ready to talk. Lee released her and stepped back, and Amanda fired a strike at her head, missing completely as Lee ducked. Lee returned the assault with a quick jab to Amanda's midsection. She gave a loud *umph* right before Lee lifted her knee solidly into the woman's face. A distinct crack of cartilage sounded before Amanda slumped to the floor. Tory ran out of her office and peered down at Amanda, who was holding two shaky hands over her face.

"What the hell happened?" Tory asked.

"Ask her," Lee said through gritted teeth.

"I've been trying to figure the same thing out for the last few minutes, Ms. West," Dan said, rubbing the back of his neck.

"Tell her, Franklin. Or I'll make it a hell of a lot worse."

"I leaked that information to the press, Ms. West." Her words were muffled by the hands held over her face, trying to catch the blood from her broken nose. "Mayfield is my uncle."

"You what!"

"I'm sorry." Amanda struggled to get to her feet and Dan assisted with a hand on her arm. "My uncle raised me from the time I was ten. He was hurting for money and I thought this story would help him out financially. I didn't realize it would get this out of hand."

Tory signaled for one of the housekeepers to bring her a towel from the kitchen and handed it to Amanda. "Franklin, you're fired. Dan?"

"Yes, ma'am?"

"Get her out of my sight." Amanda was quickly escorted away as Tory collapsed into a kitchen chair. "Lee?"

"Yes."

"I don't know what else to say. Thank you just doesn't seem enough anymore."

"As I said before, you don't need to thank me. It's my job. Now if you'll excuse me, I have a lot to do before tonight's party. Are there any last-minute changes I should be aware of?"

"No. Dan has everything," Tory said, holding up a hand to avoid Lee's next question. "Really, I promise—no more surprises."

Lee decided to do a spot check on Jo before searching out Dan and Amanda. She needed to question Amanda and find out everything she'd told Mayfield before the party. After the way her day had progressed, she seriously doubted there wouldn't be any more surprises.

CHAPTER TWELVE

Lee scanned the foyer from her position at the top of the stairs as it grew crowded with guests who huddled in small groups drinking champagne and enjoying the festive atmosphere. People had been arriving steadily all evening, making her increasingly uneasy as the crowd grew past the two-hundred mark. Jo still hadn't made an appearance.

She'd been worried about Jo ever since finding out about Amanda Franklin and had taken undetected peeks into her room as she rested. Her need to know if Jo was okay bordered on obsessive. She'd wrestled with the overwhelming urge to lie down beside her, wanting nothing more than to take Jo into her arms and shield her from anything that could possibly hurt her. But once she knew Jo was awake and preparing for the party, like a good soldier she returned to her post, moved into the shadows, and trudged forward.

Franklin's confession had kicked Lee's protective instincts into overdrive. In the service those instincts had been a large factor in her promotions. They'd helped her prepare the men under her command for battle. Those soldiers had trusted her instincts. She'd taught them how to serve with honor and protect those that needed it. But lately her feelings for Jo far surpassed a simple need to protect. The thought of harm coming to Jo scared the crap out of her. So she watched over her like an eagle protecting its nest, and if someone dared threaten her, she'd bare her talons and fight to the death.

She had no way of knowing if Jo realized how much she'd be willing to sacrifice to protect her. After the untimely muscle spasm at the restaurant, she wondered if Jo doubted her abilities, doubted her in any way. She hadn't wanted to talk about her personal life or her pain, but the look of understanding on Jo's face as she carefully traced her scar caused a familiar stirring deep inside. That touch had made her want to forget her duties, forget her promise to protect. Restraint had always been her strong point, and Jo would never know how much control it took to not surrender to that touch.

Could someone so shielded from the world appreciate what a toll the war had taken on her? War destroyed people's lives, made them value the simplest of pleasures. Could Jo ever understand what it was like to wonder if she'd wake up the next day, or if the person she was sitting next to would be dead minutes later? The more she thought about all those questions the more she realized she'd been fooling herself. Not only could Jo not understand any of those things, but she also had no idea what it was like to be trapped in a body that would forever fail her physically and mentally. She'd been surrounded by glitz and glamour, not desert sand and bombs.

The opening of a nearby door made her turn, and she tried not to gasp as she took in the most beautiful sight she'd ever seen. As Jo slowly approached, the flawless midnight-blue material swayed naturally around her lithe body. The material hugged her curves in all the right places, and even with crutches and only a hint of makeup, Jo was one beautiful woman.

Breathing evenly became more difficult as Jo slowly closed the distance between them. She dared not look into Jo's eyes, afraid she would be able to peel back another layer and leave her feeling more exposed than she already felt. She willed herself to focus as the familiar scent of coconut and lime assaulted her senses.

"Hi," Jo said shyly. "My sister tells me you're my date."

"Hello, Ms. West. And, yes. Sorry to disappoint, but we thought it would be good cover, plus it'll keep me close and not draw extra attention."

"Who said I was disappointed?" Jo locked her arm through Lee's as Lee guided her down the spiral staircase. Suddenly she stopped and tugged lightly on Lee's arm, forcing Lee to look at her. "You're not disappointed, are you?"

Lee looked at Jo, the question surprising her. Of course she wasn't disappointed. She was right where she wanted to be. And by the smile forming on Jo's face, Jo knew it too. The problem was, Jo saw too much, saw beyond the façade of who Lee pretended to be. She really did want Jo to be on her arm tonight. But she wished she didn't have to pretend to be the one by Jo's side, smiling with the knowledge that Jo wanted her and no one else in that room. She'd entertained that fantasy since Jo had bought the dress. But seeing the way people were staring at Jo, and knowing she'd never be able to completely defeat her demons, made her realize that a fantasy was all it ever would be.

She jammed her hands into her trouser pockets, trying to hide their trembling as Jo accepted a champagne glass from a passing waiter. She quickly scanned the room for anyone who looked out of place, but all seemed clear.

"Relax." Jo whispered so only Lee could hear. "We're safe."

"I'll try."

Jo slid a hand into Lee's pocket. "Hey, look at me."

Lee felt the warm fingers squeeze her hand and glanced down at Jo. She inhaled sharply. Why did Jo have to be so damn beautiful?

"I feel safe because you're with me, because I know you'd never let anything happen to me. I trust you."

"Jo…" Lee closed her eyes, allowing her words to settle over her. Trust. How could Jo trust her when she didn't even trust herself?

"Don't. I know you think I don't because of what happened at lunch. But I do. Please believe me." She gave her hand a little shake as Lee nodded. "Good. Now it's time you escort me to dinner."

"As you wish."

The dinner was excruciatingly longer than Lee had expected, and the party moved into the expansive backyard for the remaining part of the evening. Torches lined the patio like soldiers standing at attention. The illumination from the hundreds of lights offered a romantic backdrop as people danced beneath the stars. For the first time in years Lee realized how utterly alone she was. She scanned the partygoers and kept a respectful distance from Jo. If she got too close, she might not be able to move away.

"Would you dance with me?" Jo asked, turning to face Lee.

"Ms. West, I don't think—"

"You know what? Sorry. Just…forget I asked. That was out of line and not in your job description."

Jo had already turned down many subtle and not-so-subtle offers by handsome young men and an equal number of gorgeous women. Obviously, it wasn't as clear as they had meant it to be that Lee was her date. Lee let out a sigh of relief every time one of them turned dejectedly and walked away. She couldn't just sit there and ignore the tortured look in Jo's eyes. It was only one dance. What could it hurt?

"Actually, Jo, I'd be honored."

They walked to the dance floor hand in hand, moving among the gently swaying couples until they reached the middle of the floor.

A slow melody began to play and Lee held out a hand. Maybe it was the use of her first name or the intensity with which Lee was gazing at her that made Jo's voice catch in her throat. Regardless, without hesitating, she accepted the offered hand and moved into Lee's arms.

Lee's command on the dance floor shouldn't have surprised her. From what she'd learned about her so far, her need to be in control was what made her the best in the military and so good at her job. As they slowly moved in time with each other, she caught a glimpse of Tory on the other side of the room talking with Gary. She'd seen what war had done to their relationship, and what it had done to Gary's body. Recalling the look of agony on Lee's face earlier in the restaurant, she wondered if Lee's arm was bothering her now as it kept her in place, held her close.

"Is your arm okay?"

"It's fine."

"Good," Jo said, resting her head against Lee's shoulder. "Can I ask you a question?"

"Of course."

"It's personal."

"Go on," Lee whispered.

"You said outside the theater that you didn't have a lover. Is that because of what war has taken from you?"

Lee tensed. "What do you mean?"

"Well, look at Tory and Gary. I remember them as a couple before Gary was shipped off to Iraq. They had been so goo-goo eyed over each other I couldn't stand to be around them. But then he came back broken. And I don't just mean physically. He's still Gary but he's not. Something's...missing. You know what I'm saying?"

Lee closed her eyes. "You see too much."

Jo tightened her grip on Lee's neck. "I see what's important."

"Jo..." Lee stepped back, putting distance between them. "We should get back."

"Something I said?"

"No." She helped Jo back to the table and into a chair. "Sorry. If you're too close to me, I can't see around us and check for threats. Thank you for the dance. "

Jo watched Lee move to the other side of the table and tried to keep her anger in check. Why was it that every time she thought they had finally made a connection—found some common ground— Lee found a way to back away? The person she had been dancing with and who had allowed her to see her vulnerability was not the Lee Winters she had just spoken to, not the Lee she'd asked about her life and her time in the service. No, this was the bodyguard, the person who returned to the shadows because that was her duty. She wanted to ignore the heat from that burning stare coming from a few feet away. Lee was so incredibly handsome, and in that simple black tux and matching-color shirt she was without a doubt the most striking woman in the room. Jo had ached to run her fingers through that unruly dark hair, pull those tempting lips down for a kiss. But once again, Lee had subtly rebuked her—she'd made it very clear that Jo was nothing more than a paycheck.

As Lee sat across from her at the table, her gaze distant once more, Jo wanted to scream. Once again someone had proved to her that she didn't matter, that she wasn't worthy of their time or attention. Her dream that someone could look at her and only her shattered the second their dance had ended. Because the truth was, she wasn't special. Old feelings burned like acid through her veins, making her want to lash out at the one person who had done nothing but remind her that once again she was merely a casualty of her sister's life.

What a fool she was to have paid special attention to every detail from her makeup to her dress before arriving that night. She wanted to catch a glimpse of desire in Lee's eyes just like she had that afternoon in the dressing room. Lee was hot, yeah, but she was also intriguing. In the few open moments Lee allowed, Jo had glimpsed a witty, sweet woman who cared deeply about her work and her honor. That was the woman she wanted as her date tonight. Instead what she was witnessing in Lee's blank expression was disinterest, and that reality hurt worse than the injuries she'd suffered in her accident. Fine. If that's the way it was going to be then it was time to set her sights elsewhere. Someone in that room had to want her and only her, and she'd be damned if she stopped looking until she found that person.

Lee scanned the garden. She looked anywhere but directly at Jo, knowing she'd see disappointment in her eyes. She'd hated to walk away from their dance, but having Jo in her arms made her forget there were others in the room. Made her forget everything. And that put Jo's safety, as well as her own sanity, at risk.

As she continually scanned the thinning crowd a woman from earlier caught her attention. This particular woman had stolen quick glances at Jo all evening but seemed unwilling to approach. Lee had recognized her from earlier as Charlene Avery, a close personal friend of Chance Dillingham, the bass player for Total Femme. As they stood a room apart, Jo's eyes fell upon the tall blonde as she nursed a drink at the bar, and she scanned the woman in the Versace tux from head to toe. Jo smiled at the woman, giving her the go-ahead to come over. Lee's insides plummeted and her jaw ached from clenching it so tight.

The woman approached Jo and offered her arm. Jo accepted it as they left the backyard and slowly moved up the spiral staircase with Lee not far behind. As they opened the balcony doors leading out onto the veranda, Lee didn't follow, in an attempt to offer them privacy. She stayed just outside the door, far enough to not be able to eavesdrop on their conversation but close enough in case something should happen. She could hear their distinct voices, one of them unmistakably Jo's sultry alto. Her heart faltered as Jo's voice changed pitch and became even deeper, sexier.

Lee looked over her shoulder and watched as Jo wrapped her arms around the taller woman's neck. She had her head thrown back and Charlene was kissing along her jaw. When Jo angled her head to accept the offered kiss, Lee rocked backward onto her heels as if she'd been struck and the breath flew from her chest.

A wave of dizziness caused Lee to brace against the doorway as her world spiraled out of control. The vision of Jo wrapped up in someone else's arms was almost too much for her to handle. She revisited her conversation in Jo's bedroom a few weeks earlier, the term *private settings* making her gut clench as if someone was removing her stomach with a spoon. Normally, seeing two women in a passionate embrace would have been a turn-on. But that was before Jo, before she had these feelings she couldn't compartmentalize. Before now, she'd never contemplated how she'd feel seeing Jo in the arms of another woman. The reality was so much worse than she could have ever envisioned.

Her clenched fists were starting to lose feeling, and her legs were so wobbly she wasn't sure how much longer she could stand. Not able to endure the torture any longer, she took up a post just outside the door where it was impossible to see them, trying with everything in her to erase the images of Jo in that woman's embrace.

Protecting Jo was one thing, but she refused to watch her kiss another woman. She would never be strong enough for that. And as she closed her eyes and tried to block out the sounds of Jo being pleasured by someone else, Jo suddenly emerged clinging to Charlene's arm.

Helpless to interfere, Lee followed the two women as they made their way down the winding staircase, appearing as if they were going to rejoin the party. She wanted to die all over again but this time for different reasons. Her throat constricted. Her insides swelled painfully, and not in a pleasant way. She had endured a lot of pain in her life, but little could match this emptiness. And as she stood there watching Jo hang all over her escort, she felt as if someone had pulled out her heart, watching what was left of her life beat slowly in their hands.

What did you expect? You can't offer her more so it's time to pull yourself together, soldier. Do your job. She remained close but slightly out of earshot as Jo whispered something into Tory's ear. Jo never released her hold on Charlene's arm as they began to climb back up the stairs. Lee turned to follow but Tory stopped her, not looking entirely pleased.

"Jo is turning in for the night and told me to let you know she won't need your services for the rest of the evening."

Oh, God. Private matters. "Very well, ma'am. But before I go, I need to post one of the other guards outside her door in case she decides to rejoin the party," Lee said, and noticed what appeared to be a flash of sympathy in Tory's gaze.

"I understand," Tory said. "Good night, Lee."

After placing Simons in charge of Jo's security until her shift tomorrow, Lee pushed her way out the front door, the cool night air burning her lungs. She'd brave the cold, brave anything to get as far away from Jolene West as humanly possible.

As she shot through the front gate, she saw two silhouettes in a tight embrace just before the lights went out in the corner bedroom. Jo's bedroom. She'd suffer the loss and pain of nearly losing her arm all over again just to erase that one picture from her memory. Opening the throttle, she welcomed the pin-pricking sensations as the icy cool air whipped her in the face, the freezing cold matching the numbness creeping through her soul.

❖

Jo offered Charlene her throat, moaning as her teeth raked across her sensitive flesh. She ran her fingertips up Charlene's back, feeling the muscles ripple beneath the cherry-red silk shirt.

"You're so damn beautiful," Charlene whispered into Jo's ear, taking her earlobe between her teeth before sucking on the tip. "I couldn't keep my eyes off you all night."

Jo shuddered, groaning when Charlene licked her way across her shoulder. "I noticed." Charlene bit softly along Jo's collarbones, and her knees went weak when Charlene started to lightly suck on her neck. "Charlene…"

"Charlie."

Great name but not as sexy as Lee. "Charlie?"

"Hum?" Charlie mumbled as she latched onto one of Jo's nipples through the soft material.

All thought fled as Jo heard her zipper being lowered. When the dress slipped from her shoulders, she tangled her hands through Charlie's short hair and shivered when Charlie's lips molded to her nipple. Jo hissed as she nipped her tender flesh, the answering surge of pleasure pain shooting between her legs. With the material pooled at her feet, she held Charlie's lips to her breast, pushing into the inferno that was Charlie's mouth. "God! You're driving me mad."

Charlie lifted her easily and laid her on the bed. Jo lay back against the pillows as Charlie removed her clothes and crawled up next to her, clearly mindful of her injured side and cast. She reached for Charlie's head again, guiding her mouth to where it felt best.

"Yes," Jo cried, arching her back as Charlie bit, sucked, and literally licked her into a frenzy. "My underwear…please…take them off."

Charlie guided the lace bikinis carefully down Jo's hips, kissing every inch of exposed skin. "Beautiful. You smell so incredible."

Jo didn't want conversation. She wanted Charlene's hungry mouth to claim her wet center the way it had just devoured her breast. She wanted not to think for a while, and she wanted someone, anyone, to help her banish Lee's image from her mind. Charlie proved to be an excellent distraction. She covered every inch of Jo's skin with wet, warm kisses. As she began her descent and bit lightly along Jo's thigh, Jo groaned and closed her eyes. An image of Lee flashed behind her eyelids—her sexy grin, her dark eyes, the way she was always there just when Jo needed her.

Why couldn't she allow Charlie to take her, to finish what she so desperately needed? The answer was simple, even though she wished she'd picked a different time to analyze it. She covered her face with her hands, as if that could block out the image. A collage of pictures danced before her—Lee sitting by her bed, jumping in front of her at lunch earlier that day. She couldn't believe she'd allowed Lee's ghost into her bed, a bed she was sharing with another woman after far too long alone. She could hear Lee's deep laugh. She shivered at the thought of what Lee's hands could do to her body. Suddenly it occurred to her she couldn't do this with Charlie. She couldn't handle any more regrets.

"Charlie, stop. I'm sorry," Jo mumbled. "I'm so sorry. I can't do this."

Charlie reclined next to Jo, wrapping an arm around her shoulders to pull her close. She placed a gentle kiss on top of Jo's head before climbing out of bed in search of her clothes. "I understand."

How could you when I don't even understand?

Charlie pulled on her pants, avoiding Jo's gaze. "Can I ask you a question without offending you?"

"Anything." She at least owed Charlie some sort of explanation for her irrational behavior.

"Does she know?"

"Does who know what?"

"Lee," Charlie said, buttoning her shirt. "She's your bodyguard, right?"

"How did you..." Jo pulled the sheet up to cover her body, suddenly feeling exposed and foolish.

"You moaned her name right before you asked me to stop."

Jo hid her face in her hands again, feeling the heat from the blush against her palms. "Oh, my God. I'm sorry...I didn't mean..."

"Hey, look at me," Charlie said gently as she sat next to Jo on the bed and pulled Jo's hands away from her face. "I should have known better. I saw the way you two looked at each other all night, which was partly the reason I'd kept my distance from you. When you smiled at me, I was shocked. I thought maybe I'd imagined the whole thing."

"God, I feel so stupid!"

"I think we both feel a little foolish." Charlie kissed Jo on the forehead before she stood and grabbed her jacket. "Good night, Jo."

Numbness settled over her as Charlie left without another word. Jo had clearly humiliated them both, and all she wanted to do now was erase the night completely from her mind and body. She flung her head back into the pillows and let out a heavy sigh. What a complete mess she'd created, first with Lee and then with Charlie.

She had wanted Charlie at first, hadn't she? The woman's hands were magic, playing her body like a master guitarist would work the strings. It had been months since she'd been in someone else's arms. She missed the physical connection, had craved another woman's touch. But she hadn't wanted that particular woman. No, she wanted Lee, the woman who didn't want her in return. *Fantastic.*

After turning on the water for her jet tub, she covered her cast with a plastic protector before stepping into the warm water, determined to scrub the entire night away. She sobbed at her immature behavior, unable to stop her tears, and cursed her impulsiveness but didn't know any other way to act after Lee had so blatantly rebuked her. Yes, her feelings had been hurt, but instead of taking Lee's rejection like an adult, she had acted like a child and shattered the one thing that Lee valued most, someone's trust. If there was one thing Jo had learned about Lee, it was that she didn't trust easily, because she didn't feel anyone was trustworthy. Lee hid her feelings so she wouldn't have to share an essential part of herself, and just when she'd partially opened that door, Jo had slammed it in her face.

Jo cried harder, realizing she'd pushed away the first person who'd ever put her first. The only person who had put her first. Sure, she'd been paid to do so, but she had a feeling it went deeper than that with Lee. Or at least it had. She tilted her head back and let the water blend with her tears.

❖

Lee was on her third shot of tequila, lying haphazardly across her sofa. The warmth of the silver liquid helped numb her body, but nothing would be strong enough to erase the memory of Jo wrapped in another woman's arms. Instead of wiping her memory clean, each shot made the image more vivid, more intense. The glass sailed through the air, shattering into a million shards against the far wall. She reached for the phone, falling forward unsteadily.

"Shit!" She grimaced when her shin hit the coffee table. "I'm coming, damn it. Hold on." She didn't recognize the number on the caller ID. "Yeah?"

"Lee?"

Lee cleared her throat in an attempt to steady her voice and sound sober. "Hey," she said, and swayed. Christ, she couldn't think with the alcohol clouding her thoughts. Something had to be wrong for Jo to call her directly. "Everything okay?"

"Fine. Sorry to call so late. I wanted...well..."

Lee closed her eyes, wanting to say something, anything, to erase the uncertainty in Jo's trembling voice, but she had no comforting words to offer. She wasn't angry at Jo anymore, but the feelings she'd brought to the surface were too raw. She closed her eyes, feeling like a coward for what she was about to do. "Actually, Ms. West, I'm glad you called. I was going to tell you this tomorrow, but I guess now is as good a time as any."

"What is it?"

"I have another job offer and it's something I can't pass up. I hope you understand." *Resorting to lying? You really are a disgrace, soldier.*

"I see." Jo's voice was unusually controlled. Too controlled. "When do you start?"

"Monday. So I'll formally resign tomorrow. Did you need something tonight before I go?"

Lee wanted to reach through the phone and take Jo into her arms, erase the words spoken through a tequila haze. She could tell by the silence that the news wasn't sitting well with Jo, but she was both physically and mentally tired and had to hang up before she said something she'd regret.

"No. I thought it was important but it can keep until morning. Good night, Ms. Winters."

Lee kept her eyes shut tight. She could tell from the quiver in Jo's voice that she was on the edge of tears, and it killed her to know she was hurting her. But for the sake of her own sanity, she had to gain some distance. "Good night, Ms. West."

CHAPTER THIRTEEN

L ee, you can't do this," Gary said.
"Excuse me?" Lee had been pacing in her apartment for the last few hours, her nerves open and raw. After her conversation with Jo, she hadn't been able to sleep. She was tired and edgy and wasn't in the mood for any lip service from anyone. She'd called Gary the moment she thought he'd be awake.

"Look—"

"No, you *look*," she said. "I'm through, Gary. Find someone else. I don't need money this bad." *And if I have to hear or watch her practically have sex with someone again, I'll go postal.*

"But the reason I picked you—"

"I don't care about your fucking reasons. I want out—today. Fix it so she's covered and hand me my last check."

"Lee," Gary said, sighing heavily into the phone. "You know I can't just make another female bodyguard appear out of thin air, especially after that incident with Franklin. You have to give me enough time to find a replacement. It'll take at least a few weeks to find another woman with half your skills."

Did she hear right? A few weeks? Hell no. "You've got two days. By Monday I'm gone."

"Okay, okay," he said quickly. Too quickly. "I may have someone else who might be interested."

Funny, if that were true, then why didn't he use this *person* in the first place? "Who?"

"Uh…"

"Who?" Lee's tone was deadly. If it was who she thought it was, Gary wouldn't live to see tomorrow.

"Viper, but—"

"No fucking way. Understand me?" *How dare you even suggest it?* "That hotshot takes two steps in Jo's direction and I'll run her over with her own damn sports car!"

"Lee, you're not leaving me much choice. I'm outta options."

"I don't give a shit if you have to hire a Girl Scout. If I see Viper anywhere near Jo your ass is mine. Got me?"

"Yeah, yeah," he muttered.

"Good." She slammed the phone into its cradle, taking a deep breath. Viper. Jesus fucking Christ! That dishonorable poor excuse for a soldier was equivalent to a deserter, in her book. How could someone with Viper's record leave the service willingly when Lee had a chance to advance her own career and it was taken from her? She was bad news, and there was no way Lee wanted her anywhere near Jo. No matter how badly she wanted out, she couldn't quit until Gary found someone she could trust. Leaving Jo in the hands of a total stranger was inconceivable, especially since people like Amanda Franklin didn't respect or value people's privacy. What if something happened to Jo during the transition? No matter how much last night had angered and hurt her, she wouldn't put Jo's life in danger because of her personal feelings. She was a soldier, and in the sober light of day, she knew she'd have to pull herself together and suck it up no matter how much seeing Jo again would destroy her.

❖

Lee kept the face shield up on her motorcycle helmet, allowing the cool morning air to help snap her out of her hazy hangover. Between the alcohol from the night before and very little sleep, she needed something more than just a cup of coffee to jolt her awake.

She'd thought about Jo all night—recalled how beautiful she'd looked in that dress, remembered the feelings of helplessness, knowing she would never be enough for her. And then she saw her with another woman. At that moment, she knew she couldn't protect Jo any longer. Jo needed someone with a clear head, not someone whose heart was getting in the way of their duty.

She'd been so confused about her feelings for Jo before last night. She'd refused to accept that she was falling for the person she was trying to protect. But seeing Jo in Charlene's arms made her realize she was only fooling herself. She did care, more than she should. But she wouldn't put herself through that kind of pain. She wouldn't allow Jo to push her away after finding out about her demons. No, walking away before someone got hurt was better.

She twisted the throttle, the stinging sensation bringing tears to her eyes. With every mile closer to the West home, she felt a sense of dread she'd never experienced before. Yes, she'd nearly lost her life in battle, but she'd trade her life any day for the loss she was about to incur.

As she pulled into the driveway, she glimpsed someone opening the front door. She cruised to a stop just beyond the stairs and waited as Jo made her way down the front steps. She engaged the kickstand and was in the process of dismounting her bike when Jo stopped at the bottom of the stairs and leaned against a support post.

Jo waved the two bodyguards standing at the top of the stairs inside as she turned back to stare at Lee. Lee removed her gloves, shoving them into her motorcycle helmet as she approached.

"Why do you insist on driving that dangerous thing? You could get killed," Jo said, unable to keep the agitation out of her voice. Her irritation with Lee had increased since their phone call and spread like a rash through her emotions. Seeing Lee, decked out in full leathers, straddling her bike like she would a lover, made the flames and irritation burn hotter.

"I could say the same thing about you, since you really shouldn't be going down these stairs without someone's assistance."

The sexy, determined look on Lee's face made Jo forget why she was angry. Lee did strange things to her, wonderful things.

But Lee had made it very clear she would be leaving soon and obviously didn't share the same feelings. "I don't think falling down the stairs is the same as falling on that damn bike."

"You're probably right," Lee said, inching closer. "But I won't."

Jo placed her hands on Lee's jacket, intending to smooth the bent collar. The leather felt cool against her skin, but that wasn't why she was shivering. Lee's eyes were dark, dangerous in a way that made animals run from predators. They were pulling her in, holding her captive. And for the first time in forever, she didn't want to break away from her restraints. "Are you still going to leave me?" she asked in a whisper.

"Yes."

"Why?"

"Because I need to. Because I can't protect you like this. Don't you get it? I can't fight you any more, Jo."

Lee's lips were inches from her own and her whispered words set Jo's skin on fire. Her pulse raced out of control, and she was sweating even though the morning air felt cool against her skin. A pool of moisture formed between her legs as all the blood in her body rushed south.

Jo registered Lee's hands on her hips before she came to her senses and stepped back. Her crutch caught the top step, causing her to lose her balance and stumble backward. She was quickly scooped up in Lee's powerful arms and set gently back on her feet. She began to shake, and everywhere Lee's hands touched, Jo burned.

The need for Lee to rescue her again caused a flush of embarrassment to race along her cheeks. She'd wanted to believe she was independent and didn't need anyone's help. But as each day passed, she had come to rely on her shadow more and more. When was she ever going to prove, to Tory, to Lee, or more importantly to herself, that she was capable of existing without the help of others? "No wonder you're leaving. You probably think I'm a big klutz."

"You know I don't think that," Lee said softly, keeping Jo in the circle of her arms. "You've been in a terrible accident, Jo. It's understandable that your balance and your stamina haven't returned yet. But they will in time. Trust me."

Jo did trust her. She'd trusted her since the day Lee walked through her bedroom door and had become a solid presence in her chaotic life. Wrapped in Lee's arms, she wanted to kiss the lips that were inches from her own. She became lost in the hypnotic pull of Lee's eyes and slowly bent forward, her heartbeat thundering in her ears. She wanted, needed, Lee—and no one else.

"Please," Jo whispered, her lips a breath from Lee's.

"Yes."

Jo didn't know what had caused her heart to pound more violently. Was it the look of longing on Lee's face or was it the shock of a loud engine that yanked her out of the moment? She stepped away from Lee's embrace as a bright-yellow sports car sped through the front gate and pulled alongside Lee's bike.

"Jo!"

Jo's chest heaved and her legs barely kept her upright as she squinted into the morning sun, barely recognizing the woman waving at her frantically from a convertible Lamborghini Murcielago.

"Patricia!" Jo waved as the lead guitarist for Total Femme ran up the front steps, swooping Jo off her feet.

Patricia Simpson was not only one of the best female guitarists in the country, but also the second most popular member of the group, next to Tory. Jo hadn't seen Patricia since the group's last tour had ended nearly six months ago. They tended to hang out a lot when the group was on tour, probably because Patricia had always liked Jo more than Tory. Patricia also sought out female companionship, so when touring, Jo and Patricia spent a lot of their time frequenting female clubs, most of the time just talking with each other well into the night. Patricia was a few years older than Jo and more aggressive when it came to women, but she'd always kept an eye on Jo when they were out, treating her like the little sister she'd never had.

"I'm *so* sorry I couldn't get here after your accident. I was in France on holiday when Tory called to tell me. How are you, darling?" Patricia said, turning Jo's face to get a better look at her.

"Better, but I'm getting restless. I feel trapped in this big house, and now I have my own bodyguard to keep me company at all times, thanks to Tory."

Patricia lowered her Coach sunglasses to the end of her nose to look at Lee, who had taken up post next to the front door in an effort to afford the women privacy. The predatory look in Patricia's eyes was hard to ignore as she did everything but wet her lips. "My, my, and just where did your sister find that hunk of a woman?" Patricia nearly purred, scanning the leather-clad figure up and down.

Jealousy surged through Jo's body even though she should have anticipated Patricia's reaction. Seeing Patricia eye Lee like a hungry tiger stalking a gazelle made her want to growl a friendly warning for Patricia to keep her distance. However, she held no claim on Lee and wondered what Lee thought about the striking and irresistible Total Femme guitarist.

"Would you like me to introduce you?" Jo asked as she reluctantly led Patricia toward the house.

The look in Patricia's eye was feral. "But of course, darling. Lead on."

Thankfully, the introductions were kept short and Jo led Patricia into Tory's study. They all gathered around the stone fireplace, awaiting Tory's arrival. When Tory finally appeared, she was in the process of removing a brunette wig and contacts that were part of her onstage persona. Marilyn had explained she'd just returned from taping at a popular late-night TV show and that the episode would air Monday night.

"My God, Tory, you look terrific, as always." Patricia accepted Tory's quick peck on the cheek. "How did the taping go? Oh, and did you see those new costumes they want us to wear for the tour? Ghastly, I tell you."

Tory laughed. "Thanks. You look great too. The taping went fine and those costumes are horrendous. I really need to talk to Marilyn about the lace, or lack thereof."

"Hear, hear." Patricia obviously agreed.

"I'm glad you finally made it," Tory said, pouring drinks at the bar. "You missed quite a party last night."

"So I heard from Darian," Patricia said. "Was she the only other band member who attended? I forgot to ask her on the phone this morning."

"Yes. You know how the others are when we're not touring."

"That I do." Patricia accepted the glass from Tory with a nod of thanks. "I'm also sorry I missed the press conference. Is that mess all cleared up?"

"Yes, but unfortunately there have been some other developments. I'm sure the details would only bore you, but if you want some excitement, ask Jo about last night."

Jo bowed her head to avoid everyone's eyes, wanting to strangle her sister with the scarf she wore around her neck. No way would she discuss this topic in front of Lee, especially since they'd almost kissed right out on the front steps less than ten minutes earlier.

"Who was she, Jo?" Patricia asked. "Anyone I know?"

"No…no one."

"Oh, come on, Jo. What's with all the secrecy?" Tory asked. "Charlene Avery is—"

"Tory—"

"Charlene Avery." Patricia whistled in surprise. "My, my. I've been trying to get Chance's friend into my bed for years, but that gorgeous butch wouldn't give me the time of day. What's your secret?"

Acting like an immature idiot helps. "Can we drop this?" She finally chanced a look at Lee, but her posture was as inflexible as a piece of steel, and her expression was so blank her face might as well have been carved of marble.

"Well, I'm sure you both had fun and you can tell me all about it later," Patricia said. "How about we have lunch at Martidi's and you both can catch me up on current events? Come, come, my treat."

Jo wanted to shed her skin and crawl into a hole. Thank God Patricia was smart enough to pick up on the tension in the room. She'd always been a good friend to Jo, and, unlike Tory, she knew how to be discreet when the situation called for it. She'd have to make it a point to thank her later. "Sounds good to me."

"Wonderful." Patricia grabbed her purse. "Let's go."

The entourage climbed into Tory's stretch limo, which was able to carry all three of them plus three bodyguards, with room to spare. They reached the familiar restaurant within the hour, the conversation sparse, with Jo not wanting to discuss anything that had happened last night with Lee in such close proximity, especially the part where Lee was planning to leave. They hadn't had a chance to talk about it yet, and she really hoped she could come up with some way to change her mind. Funny, a few months ago, the idea of having a bodyguard pissed her off. Now she couldn't imagine not having Lee in her life.

They managed to get a private table in the back of the popular Italian restaurant, with the bodyguards sitting behind them at their own table but within reach.

Jo tried relaxing, but every so often she glanced in Lee's direction and saw her pushing the food around on her plate. For a brief moment their eyes met and she nearly gasped out loud at the unmistakable look of desire in Lee's eyes.

"So, Jo," Patricia said, pulling Jo's attention away from Lee's penetrating gaze. "Will you be accompanying us on tour?"

"No, not this time."

Tory halted the fork halfway to her mouth. "Jo, I thought we'd put this issue to rest. I need you."

"No. That's what you want to think. I told you yesterday that I'm leaving in a month."

"I can't believe you'd rather go to Kauai alone instead of travel with us to Europe. I mean, who'd do that? You can be so damn stubborn sometimes! And how am I supposed to manage my schedule without you?"

"What a control freak! Other stars manage to live a celebrity life without a twin. You can too."

"Ladies," Patricia said, "no fighting in public."

"Fine." Jo threw her napkin onto the table. "I need to use the restroom."

Jo disappeared into the bathroom and Lee moved discreetly closer to the door, glad she could still hear the conversation between the two band members from where she stood. Eavesdropping wasn't exactly polite, but the conversation involved Jo, and she wanted to know what they were thinking. Tory mumbled some unintelligible words, swallowing them along with a few sips of white wine.

"Well, I see nothing's changed," Patricia said with a bit of humor.

"No, but she'll eventually come around and see that this is best for everyone."

"For everyone or for you?"

Exactly! Maybe Tory would finally understand that touring wasn't in Jo's best interest, especially while she was healing.

"You have something to say to me, Patricia?"

"Look, I don't want to step out of line, but since you asked, it seems that even after all these years you still don't understand the emotional complexity of your twin."

"How would you know?" Tory said angrily. "You haven't seen her in months."

"True, but it doesn't take a rocket scientist to figure out what she wants. Think about it, Tory. Look at it from her perspective and what do you see?"

"I hate it when you play psychologist. All I see is someone who doesn't appreciate the opportunities handed to her."

"And those would be what?"

"Look around you," Tory said dramatically, with a sweep of her hand. "We have everything. Fame. Money. She'll never go without. What more could she possibly need?"

"I think you know the answer to that," Patricia said. "You just don't want to accept it."

"Okay, enough! I've had enough of this psychoanalysis bullshit. Why don't you go see what's taking Jo so long."

❖

Lee leaned against the bathroom door, waiting anxiously for Jo to reappear. Tory had left Patricia sitting alone at the table when she had stormed out minutes earlier, mumbling something about Jo being stubborn. After ten long minutes of waiting impatiently, Lee went in. Jo had her back to the wall, her arms wrapped around herself as she cried. She pulled Jo into her arms and held her while she sobbed. "Are you all right?"

"No. I'm never going to be all right. She just doesn't get it. Why can't she understand that I'm not her? That I don't want this life anymore."

"Shh, it's okay."

"Is it?"

Lee kissed Jo's forehead in reassurance before placing a few more kisses on her tear-stained cheeks and tracing her lips with the tip of her thumb. "Yes, it is."

"Please," Jo whispered for the second time that day. "I need you to kiss me."

Lee trembled and groaned as what remained of her control slipped away like Jo's silky hair through her fingertips. The first full meeting of their lips nearly took her breath away, and as she deepened the kiss, she parted Jo's lips with her tongue, wanting to devour Jo until there was nothing left.

At first, she'd intended the kiss to calm Jo, to use her lips as a balm to soothe Jo's aching heart. She couldn't stand to see her suffering and she would have kept Jo in her arms forever, but the bathroom door swung open.

"Jo, are you okay—" Patricia stopped short. "Whoops."

Lee released Jo and stepped back, feeling the fragile bond between them snap. In a surprisingly steady voice Jo said, "I'm fine. Where's Tory?"

"Outside still, I think. Should I go tell her you're..." Patricia glanced at Lee. "Busy?"

"No. I'll be right out."

Lee excused herself and pushed through the bathroom door, refusing to look at either of them. Holy fuck! She'd just gotten caught kissing her client—the woman she was being paid to protect—in a bathroom, of all places, like some stupid teenager. It was official. She'd finally lost her mind. Nothing else made sense. She'd taken advantage of Jo during an emotional moment, and she could only hope Jo could find a way to forgive her.

The silence was thick between them for the rest of the day. They had driven back home and Jo had returned to the solitude of her room. After posting Simons outside Jo's door, Lee went in search of Tory. She hadn't thought of anything for the past few hours except finding some way to apologize for her unprofessional behavior. But she didn't want to apologize, and if Patricia hadn't shown up when she did, Lee would have ripped down a barrier that would have been impossible to resurrect. If, in fact, there was any barrier left to speak of.

"Ms. West," Lee said to Tory, who had just emerged from her study. "May I speak with you a moment?"

"Of course. Why don't you come in and take a seat." She motioned with her head toward her office.

"Thanks, but I'd rather stand," she said, moving in front of Tory's desk while waiting for her to sit.

"This seems serious."

"I'm afraid it is, ma'am. Has Gary talked to you about my resignation?"

"Yes," she said with a sigh. "And let me tell you, Lee, I'm not pleased. I had hoped you would change your mind. I've said it before. Jo trusts you and I don't know what's going on, but if it's the money we can pay you more."

Christ, if that was only the problem they wouldn't be having this conversation. And the Jo-trusting-her comment was like taking a dagger to the heart. "No, ma'am. It's not about money."

"Then what is it?"

I want to sleep with your sister, and I don't know how many times I can put on the brakes.

"Look...Lee," Tory said, obviously exasperated. "I'm not blind. I've seen the way my sister looks at you and you at her. I've been with a soldier. I know about duty. And I know you'll do the right thing when it comes to Jo. You'll protect her because she needs you."

Lee had thought of nothing but that kiss since they'd returned home. How she wanted to pull Jo back into her arms and finish what they'd started. And now, Tory was telling her she could forget all about that and find the focus to be the strength and presence that Jo needed. Could she really be that honorable? No. She wanted her too badly, and that compromised Jo's safety.

"Even so, ma'am. Gary will find you a replacement by Monday. I'm going to check on your sister and then head home for the night. I'm sorry."

After placing a permanent guard outside of Jo's door and calling Gary to make sure he'd found a decent replacement, she climbed onto her bike and headed home. Forty-eight more hours and she could leave this chapter of her life behind her and forget everything that Jo had come to mean to her. It was exactly what she'd asked for, so why did it hurt so much?

CHAPTER FOURTEEN

Jo stared at her x-rays through teary eyes. Doctor Chase had determined her anklebones weren't healing as fast as he'd hoped. Another cast wouldn't be necessary, but she would inherit a boot and a cane for the next four weeks, with physical therapy to follow. As he wrote out her new prescription, she felt like he might as well have been signing her death warrant.

"But you said I'd be healed by now," Jo said, finally reaching her breaking point—exhaustion and frustration had gotten the better of her. Sleep had completely eluded her the night before, Lee's imminent departure playing in her thoughts. The only positive thing she had to look forward to was having the cast removed. But even that hope was gone and she would be dependent on help for yet another four weeks. That meant she probably couldn't handle Kauai on her own, either.

"That's not what I said, Jo," he said gently. "I said the casts would come off in six to eight weeks. You have to wear this brace to protect the bones for a little while longer. Come on, it's not so bad. In about a month you won't even need the brace."

She stared at the vinyl boot complete with two metal bars that ran vertical from her ankle to mid-calf. She jumped as he secured the snaps in place, a harsh reminder that she was still a prisoner of her sister's life no matter how anyone tried to sugarcoat it.

"Is someone waiting for you in the lobby to take you home?"

"Yes, my bodyguard."

"Tory isn't here with you?" he asked in surprise. "Should I call her?"

"No, that's okay. I can do things without her." Jo hadn't wanted to tell Tory about the appointment because she wanted to prove she was ready to figuratively and literally stand on her own two feet. After their argument at lunch yesterday, she was ready to retake control of her life and move forward. Now, between the brace and physical therapy, that would all have to wait.

Doctor Chase stood and handed her a tissue and a prescription. "You're free to go. Give this to the nurse on the way out if you need it. Oh, and don't forget. Make an appointment with one of my staff for four weeks from today."

Jo accepted the wooden cane and hobbled out of the office. Lee immediately looked at the boot and the cane and rose to offer her assistance. Unable to cope by herself any longer, she rested her head on Lee's shoulder and cried, the warmth from Lee's arms wrapped around her a welcome comfort.

"Hey, hey, come on. Tell me," Lee said tenderly, guiding Jo to one of the plastic chairs.

"Four more weeks." She nearly choked on the lump in her throat.

"Is there something I can do?"

"No, there's nothing anyone can do. I need to get away from all this, and since going to Kauai will have to wait now, I need to come up with an alternate plan," she said as Lee tensed. "I don't think I can endure staying in that house until I'm healed. I have to get away before I snap under this pressure."

"And when did you decide to go to Kauai?"

"When I met with my friend Emily. I only just told my sister, but she blew me off as usual."

"I see," Lee said, staring into the distance, the familiar tightening of her jaw returning.

"Hey, are *you* okay?" Jo asked, squeezing Lee's hand to get her attention.

"Yeah…sorry. Spaced for a second."

"Not so fast." Jo grabbed Lee's arm to keep her from rising. "I've seen that look before. What were you thinking?"

Lee sighed. "I understand how you feel because I've been there. Living with pain is not something we choose. But I promise, it will get easier with time."

"Are we talking physical or emotional?"

"Both," Lee said, offering Jo her hand. "Come on. It's been a long morning. How about breakfast? It's still early."

"Sure. But you will eat *with* me, right? Like sit across the table and converse, not stand in some corner while I choke down a piece of toast."

"Jo," Lee said, closing her eyes. "I don't think—"

"No." Jo placed her hand on Lee's chest. "You don't get a say this time. I only have a few more hours with you before you leave me. Please. Don't say no. Not today." *I need you.*

Lee shuddered and opened her eyes. "Let's eat then."

❖

Jo called Emily the minute she returned home. She cried as she explained about the boot she had to wear and that her plans for Kauai would have to wait a few more months. She cried for all her disappointments but, most of all, because Lee's time as her bodyguard was ticking away.

Lee had been quiet during their breakfast, refusing to relay any details about her mysterious new job. Every time Jo asked, Lee changed the subject, asking her if she was feeling okay or if there was anything she could do. Begging Lee to stay occurred to her more than once. She wanted to tell her that even though she didn't want a babysitter at first, she couldn't imagine not having Lee in her life after today. But begging would only make things worse, and she hated the pain and despair visible in Lee's eyes. She didn't want to make it worse by being selfish.

Alone. A concept she was familiar with. Well, not anymore. After today she refused to come in second to anyone. She would have to find a more direct way to get her autonomy back and build her life around her own needs. Maybe then someone could love her for her.

She angrily swiped at her tears as a knock on the door broke the silence. She didn't even have time to say "come in" before Tory entered the room and pulled Jo into her arms.

"I heard. Tell me everything."

At any other time in the last few years, Jo would have pushed Tory away and told her to get the hell out. Instead she returned the hug and let the tears come.

"Oh, honey," Tory said gently. "I'm so sorry. I should have been there for you. I'm just so busy getting ready for the tour."

"I don't want your pity," Jo said, shoving Tory away. "For once this is about me, Tory. Me! I'm done being the wounded animal in a cage."

"What are you saying?"

"I'm *saying* that I refuse to live like this anymore. Maybe Kauai is out for now, but I can get an apartment somewhere until I'm healed. I can't be here anymore. I just can't." Jo hobbled to the closet and grabbed an overnight bag, filling it quickly with essentials.

"Wait, please wait." Tory grabbed Jo's hand. "I can't let you walk out of here. You're not even fully healed."

"You don't have a choice," Jo said, yanking her arm away. "Now get out and leave me alone."

"No, damn it. Not while he's still out there."

"I don't care anymore. Besides, my bodyguard's leaving, and you're planning on touring. Once again, everyone's getting on with their life but me. It's time that all changes."

"You know," Tory said, her rising temper evident by the flush in her cheeks. "How can you be so selfish? If you just toured with us, we wouldn't have to split up. We wouldn't need all these damn bodyguards because we would be together and I wouldn't have to worry about you all the time."

Jo began to laugh. She couldn't help it. Once again, Tory had turned the conversation around to be about her. "You're incredible.

All you've ever cared about is yourself—your career, your looks, your talent, your feelings. What about me, Tory? What about what I want, what I feel?"

"I do care about those things. Why do you think I made you my manager in the first place and gave you everything you ever wanted or needed? No matter what you think, all I've ever wanted was for you to be happy."

"Oh, really? Then I'm going to let you in on a little secret. You're going to get your wish. I'm going to be happy and I'm getting out of here to do it."

"Jo, please—"

"Just get out. Out!" Tory turned and brushed past Lee, who had taken it upon herself to enter. Jo could feel Lee's eyes on her but didn't have the strength to face another disappointment. "You too. I need to be alone."

"Not until I know you're all right."

"I'll never be all right." Jo wasn't going to pretend that any part of her current situation was okay, especially the part where Lee would be leaving, never to return. She'd never wanted a bodyguard—still didn't. What she wanted was the person standing in her doorway, the person who always looked at her as if no one else mattered, looked at her as someone she desired, not someone she protected. "Besides, why do you care? You're just like her. I'm not someone for you to command, to control. Just leave. It'll save us both the good-byes."

Looking over her shoulder wasn't necessary to know when Lee had left. The emptiness had returned, a feeling of loss so deep she shivered from the coldness that engulfed her. She buried her face in her hands and cried. The tears fell like rain for her parents, for her damaged relationship with her sister, and for the accident that had left her broken and dependent. But most of all her heart bled for the way things had ended with Lee. She was walking out of Jo's life and taking a piece of her soul with her.

❖

Lee burst through the door of Tory's office and looked at the letter clutched in Tory's shaking hands. "Ms. West, let me see." She scanned the letter quickly, her heart threatening to beat through her chest.

Tonight was a warning. You will meet me or your twin is next. The clock is ticking. You know where to find me. I await you, my love.

She darted from the room and ran up the stairs, taking them two at a time. She burst through Jo's bedroom door, catching Jo in the process of slinging her overnight bag over her shoulder.

"I thought you'd left." Jo said, her tone resigned, weary.

"I did but…" Lee didn't have time to finish her sentence when her cell phone rang. "I'm sorry. I have to take this. Winters," she said tightly.

"What's happened?" Jo asked as soon as Lee ended the call.

"That was Gary. Amanda Franklin is dead."

Jo gasped and paled. "How?"

"Someone blew up her apartment, with her in it."

"Oh, God. Lee, my sister—"

Tory burst through the door followed closely by Dan Powers.

"Did you know?" Jo asked Tory.

"I just found out."

"But why is this maniac doing this? He didn't know Amanda. Hell, we barely knew her."

"He must have found out she was the one who leaked the information to Mayfield." Tory was clearly distraught, her hands shaking and the color leached from her face. "He's doing this because I won't agree to meet with him. It's obvious she was an example, Jo, just like you were."

Lee caught the flash of lightning in Jo's blue eyes before her anger surfaced. It seemed that someone had finally paid with their life for Tory's refusal to deal with this potential threat.

"Are you happy now?" Jo asked Tory.

"Oh, my God. How can you ask that? You think I wanted this?"

"No, I don't think that. But you're so wrapped up in your own life you don't see how your actions affect others. You refused to call in the police because you didn't want to damage your precious career, and now someone's dead. You didn't stop when he nearly killed me, and that was bad enough. Now he *has* killed someone, and that's your fault. I'm sorry about Amanda, but you're done having any say in my life." Jo slung the bag over her shoulder as the cab she'd requested honked his horn out front. She tried leaving but Lee successfully blocked the doorway. "Get out of my way."

"No. Please don't leave," Lee said, panic evident in her voice.

"What is it? Now what are you both not telling me?"

"Ma'am, please..." Lee said, her eyes locked on Tory's in a desperate plea to fill in the blanks. "Jo, hear me out," Lee said, placing her hand on Jo's arm to get her attention. "We have to keep you protected more now than ever. The stalker has killed Amanda, and if Tory doesn't answer the letter she's just received he'll... he'll..."

Tory slumped into a chair. "He'll come after you again."

"Wait, what letter?" Jo said.

"I received another letter a few minutes ago," Tory said. "He says I know where to find him. What the hell does that mean? Why would I know that? And that Amanda was a wake-up call. If I don't meet him the next time, he promised he'd kill you."

Jo swayed as Lee reached for her and pulled her into her arms.

"Jesus Christ! But...who will..." Jo couldn't voice her needs.

"Protect you?" Jo nodded against Lee's chest. "I believe I'm still your bodyguard. That is...if you still want me to be?"

CHAPTER FIFTEEN

W hy are you pacing, you fool?"
The Angry Man had just returned from his greatest
triumph yet. Adrenaline coursed through his body and he needed
a way to burn off the excess energy. He'd been on a high ever
since that bodyguard's home blew to tiny pieces. The only thing
he regretted was not being given the opportunity to sift through
the rubble for any information on Tory. Amanda had to have had a
folder, pictures, something that she had been able to copy and hand
over to her uncle, that foul little reporter. A new picture would
have been a treasure to add to the multitude of others on his wall,
a small token to remind him of his greatest accomplishment so far.
"You know why. Didn't you see what I've done? I'm brilliant!"
"The explosion was incredible. I'll give you that."
"Yes," he said, pulling at his hair and ripping out a few strands
in the process. "Maybe now she'll listen to me."
He moved frantically around the small room, mumbling
incoherently. Tory would have to take him seriously now. He'd
killed someone for her. Amanda's death should have proved how
much he loved her, how much he was willing to risk for her love in
return, how far he'd go to keep her and never let her go.
"So what's next?"
He glanced at his tormentor, the crazed eyes staring boldly
back at him. They were dark, lifeless, empty of any emotion. He

hated how those eyes could see into his soul. He couldn't hide from them no matter how hard he tried. "I told you, I've made my point. Now I'll convince her to see me! All she has to do is follow the fucking instructions." He kicked a chair across the room, then chased it. Picking it up, he held it above his head before slamming it repeatedly against the floor until he'd exhausted himself.

"And this is why I call you an idiot," his tormentor hissed. "You're always pissed off. You lack focus...self-control, like a child throwing a tantrum when he doesn't get what he wants."

"Fuck off!" He moved to his desk to finish the last of his preparations before heading out to meet the woman who consumed his every moment, both waking and dreaming. He took one last look in the mirror, regretting his mistake instantly.

"Where are you going?"

"I told you already. Why do you torture me?"

The man laughed. He always laughed. "Because it's too easy. Besides, you're pathetic, or haven't I told you lately?"

"You just wait." The Angry Man scowled and pointed at him. "You'll see. After tonight I'll prove my worth to you and to her." He pulled the tattered picture from his pocket and kissed the faded image of the woman staring back at him. He saw the love in her eyes. She smiled only for him.

"Oh." The man mocked him, he always mocked him. "You still think she's going to show, don't you?"

He grabbed the paperweight on his desk. He didn't want to be tormented tonight. Not tonight. "I told you, she will show!"

Launching the paperweight into the mirror, he laughed as it shattered it into a million pieces. "Now, maybe you'll shut up and listen to *me*." He kicked a piece of the mirror with his foot.

CHAPTER SIXTEEN

Chaos descended upon the West household, and Jo tried adjusting to the constant police presence following Amanda's death. She'd actually started wishing for the days when she'd had to deal with only one bodyguard. Agitated was too mild for what she was feeling. Pissed off with people in her personal space was more like it. But she had blamed Tory for Amanda's death, and now she had to deal with the consequences. Tory had gone straight downstairs and called the police.

And, of course, the local authorities called the FBI to request their assistance with the stalker situation. In addition to not having the manpower on the local level, they needed the FBI's expertise in the handling of these types of cases. Tory handed over every letter and talked with agents for hours on end. Jo didn't want any part of those conversations. Mentally she was on overload and didn't need the added stress, particularly after she heard Tory's idea about trying to set up a meeting with the stalker in an attempt to draw him into the open.

"Are you crazy? You don't know what this guy is liable to do."

"Jo," Tory said calmly, "no one else can do this. I have to do something or you'll be in danger again. You just don't know…"

Jo didn't need to hear the words to understand what her sister was trying to say. Tory had already proved by planning to meet with the stalker that she'd risk everything, including her own life, to protect her and those she cared about from further danger. "I'm not letting you do this."

"Jo, we don't have a choice. Besides, you're leaving anyway."

"But that's not..." *Not what...true? Yesterday I had one foot out the door.* No matter how mad she was at Tory, she couldn't leave now. Tory was in danger. She needed to make her see that no matter how much she hated her life, she didn't hate Tory.

"You were saying?"

"I was saying that I've decided to stay. I can't let you do this. Damn it, I love you. Don't you get it?" Tears clouded her eyes and she wiped them away with the back of her hand. Tory came to her and wrapped her up in her arms.

"I love you too. I'm so sorry, Jo, for everything. For hiding all this, for your accident, for getting Amanda killed—"

"No!" Jo hugged her tight and whispered, "You didn't kill Amanda. I know that's what I said, but I was angry at you. I've been angry with you since the night Mom and Dad died. I know that wasn't your fault either, but you'd begged them to come to your concert. It was Chicago in the middle of winter, for Christ's sake, but still they could never turn you down. They died on that road alone, Tory. And when the concert was over, you hopped onto the next plane to London and left me to deal with the aftermath. You said it was because you couldn't cope with it, but I know that emotionally detached routine you want others to buy is bullshit. I know their deaths weren't your fault either, but that still didn't make it any easier for me. You left me alone. I don't want to end up like Mom and Dad, somewhere alone. But I'll deal with my issues when this nightmare is over. I know you would never intentionally hurt someone, but you can be very self-absorbed sometimes. I'll stay, for now. But we're in this together. Okay?"

Tory pulled back and wiped at her own eyes with her sleeve. "Just sometimes?"

"Don't push it." Jo smiled. "Now back to this stalker crap. They can try to capture this psycho whack job any way they see fit, but you are not going to risk your life. They can find another way. Maybe we can leave early for the tour—get away from all this craziness?"

"You mean you'll go?"

"What part of we're in this together did you not get? Where you go, I go. Touring, the upcoming book signing, all of it."

"But Jo. You don't need to be at the book signing. Touring is fine—"

"Jesus! You just don't get it, do you? No one, not you, not Lee, or even psycho fucking letter writer is going to dictate what I will and will not do from now on. I want to support you and be there for you. And I will be. So deal with it."

That one conversation wouldn't repair all the frayed strings that had once securely bound them together, but it was a start. They'd both come to an understanding that neither one wanted to be away from the other during this trying time. Jo found it amazing that a few days ago she had planned on leaving. Now running away was the furthest thing from her mind. And somehow, making that decision gave her a sense of control. She was staying because she wanted to, not at someone else's whim. And for whatever reason, that made a big difference.

"Fine." Tory put her hands up in defense. "You win."

"Don't I always?" Jo grinned and left.

Just moments later she found Lee staring over a couple of documents spread out on the kitchen table. "Hey, do you know where Tory went? We were talking and I left for one minute and she disappeared."

"Her office," Lee said, placing her hands in her pants pockets. "They're trying to decide what to do about the event tonight. How are you holding up?"

"Okay. If I could sleep more than two hours a night I'd probably feel better."

Lee leaned against the table and studied Jo with her usual bruising intensity. Jo wanted to go to her, to wrap her arms around Lee's waist and bury herself in those strong arms. She missed that simple comfort, but since the police and FBI had arrived, Lee had been even more distant, and Jo had to respect that distance even though she didn't like it.

"You'll try and rest later, won't you?" Lee asked.

"I'll try," Jo said, but she was too wrapped up in the way Lee's eyes darkened to say anything else.

"Jo," Lee whispered, moving away from the desk and closer to her.

"I know."

"What do you know?"

"I know," she said, putting her hands on Lee's waist, "that when this is all over, we need to talk. When I'm no longer your job, I hope to be something else to you."

Lee's eyes softened, the look of longing in them nearly bringing Jo to her knees. Lee pulled her into a tight embrace. "I promise, we'll talk then," she whispered against Jo's temple.

"That's good enough. Come on. I actually want to go see what the FBI has to say, and I'm sure you do too."

They found Tory still in her office talking with two of the FBI's finest. Jo immediately took stock of the men sitting across from her. Both wore the required dark suit, monochromatic tie, and polished black shoes. The larger of the two men, Special Agent in Charge Sam Steele, made her feel anything but safe with the look of indifference he threw her way. He looked…bored. The only person that ever made her feel safe was propped against the wall directly behind her. She didn't have to turn around to know Lee was focused on her. She could feel the warmth from that penetrating stare all the way to her toes and listened carefully as Tory explained about the tour and her hopes of the stalker fading into the background. The FBI, however, didn't share her sentiment.

"Ms. West," Agent Steele said. "Amanda Franklin's death made it clear that this man is serious. His letter requests you meet him tonight. If you help us out, we will guarantee your safety. If you decide not to meet him, he's likely to kill again."

Jo crossed her arms. "Not happening."

Tory smiled and grasped Jo's hand. "You heard my sister. So what are our other options?"

"We wait," he said, his displeasure with Tory's decision obvious. "For the time being, I would like to add a few agents to your staff."

"Is that really necessary?" Jo said.

"Yes, ma'am, it is. Your bodyguards aren't enough. I'm sure they know their jobs, but we're trained professionals and better equipped to handle these types of situations. They don't have the tools or the ability to deal with a problem of this caliber."

Maybe it was the way he said it. Maybe it was his tone or the fact that he dared disregard Lee's ability with a simple shrug or that shit-eating, patronizing grin. Whatever it was, she'd heard enough. "Agent Steele, I'm sure my sister agrees with me on this. We appreciate your help with this matter, but I have one bodyguard and I don't want another. You all work this out among yourselves. And Tory," she said, turning to her, "let me know what the plan is after while."

"Okay, talk to you later."

Jo rose from her chair, refusing to break eye contact with Agent Asshole. She'd had enough of his arrogant, macho attitude and didn't care how big the man was. If he so much as hinted again that Lee wasn't capable, she'd take a stab at trying to knock out one of those pearly whites.

"I can't believe this," she said, moving into the living room with Lee in tow. She sank onto the sofa as Lee moved to the dining table to retrieve a few documents. The word *edible* came to mind as she caught Lee bending over the table wearing her usual pair of Levi's, black boots, and a tight black T-shirt. It took all of her restraint not to jump her where she stood.

"What's not to believe?" Lee sat next to her and gently squeezed her knee. "Look, I know you're stressed but it will be all right."

"How can you say that?"

"Look at me. You have to trust me. I won't let anything happen to you. And the FBI is doing what they do best, even if they're a pain in the ass." Lee softly ran her thumb over Jo's lower lip.

It took all of Jo's control not to take that thumb into her mouth and suck on the tip of it until Lee either pulled away or surrendered. Suddenly the past few days became a blur. Her hands shook where they rested on Lee's bare forearms. The muscles beneath her fingertips twitched. She licked her lips, eyeing the trickle of sweat that coursed down the side of Lee's neck. When it passed over Lee's rapid pulse point, the dam burst. Leaning forward, she licked it away. Lee groaned.

The taste of Lee ignited a spark that set her entire body on fire. She was slowly becoming engulfed in sexual heat—every nerve ending in her body screamed for Lee's cool tongue to put out the flames. Lee gasped as Jo's fingers played up and down her arms. She knew exactly what she was doing to her, and it didn't appear Lee had the strength to pull away anymore. Lee touched Jo's face and traced the length of the thin scar beneath her eye. She shuddered, and then, trembling all over, she grabbed Lee's shoulders.

The sound of footsteps out in the hallway caught their attention and Lee pulled away.

Lee straightened, needing distance from Jo. She wanted Jo more than she wanted air to breathe, but now was not the time. The stalker was still out there and that knowledge left her feeling helpless. She couldn't do this now, not with so much at stake. She slowly withdrew, even though her body was screaming at her to reengage and finish what they'd started.

"Why do you always pull away from me?" Jo said sadly.

"I'm sorry," Lee said, unable to look at her. "I have other things to do."

Lee moved to the door but Jo stepped in front of her, blocking her exit. Lee almost laughed at the idea of Jo using herself as a barricade, considering she could bench more than twice Jo's weight. But the defiant stance and the fire in Jo's eyes made her heart rate double.

"I'm sorry but I thought I was your *thing*," Jo said thickly, placing her hands firmly on Lee's chest.

"You are." Lee held Jo's hands tight against her body. Just an inch to the left or right and she'd be begging Jo to touch her.

"Then why won't you talk to me? Let me in? You keep pulling away at a time when what I really need is for you to pull me close. I see the ghosts in your eyes. What are you hiding from?"

Lee flashed back to a time when death and destruction were a part of her daily life. Losing people, especially people under her command, had nearly cost her what was left of her sanity. When she thought about what could happen after Tory ignored the UNSUB's last request, thoughts of losing Jo rendered her powerless. Suddenly her legs shook and she rested against the door for support. "Jo, give me a second."

"Stop. I'm the only one here. It's okay," she whispered, stroking the sweat-soaked hair away from Lee's eyes. "No one will see you like this, I promise. Just tell me what happened."

Lee moved to the couch and sat with her head bowed and her arms dangling between her legs. "I was remembering the war and the loss of my troops. Then I thought about…about…"

"Hey, come on. I'm here. Tell me."

"I thought about something happening to you." Lee finally looked at her. "It scared me."

Jo couldn't think of anything on earth that could possibly frighten a woman of Lee's caliber, but the admission brought a new round of tears to her eyes. "And it scared you because of—what? Because it's your job to protect me?"

"It used to be."

"Used to be? But I thought…"

"What I mean is, it isn't *just* about my job anymore."

Lee kissed Jo, a brief kiss full of meaning and want. She knew of no other way to explain to Jo that she wasn't going anywhere. Jo's obvious sigh of relief proved that another barrier had disintegrated all around them. When she opened her eyes, she smiled regretfully at Jo.

"Don't," Jo whispered. "You know I feel the same way."

"But we shouldn't…"

"Don't." Jo whispered more fiercely, wrapping her arms around Lee's waist and laying her head against her strong chest. "Just…don't."

CHAPTER SEVENTEEN

L ee paced her apartment, feeling uptight and a little wild. She couldn't believe she'd kissed Jo—again. Or that she'd nearly fainted in her arms and told her things that she should never have admitted. Some soldier she was. What a disgrace.

The bottle of tequila sitting on the nightstand was the apple in her Garden of Eden. Struggling to resist the temptation she took slow deliberate breaths in an attempt to calm her racing heart. She couldn't risk a drink when she'd promised she'd be back at Jo's within the hour. Breaking her word wasn't an option, and she swore she wouldn't allow her fears to convince her to do it now.

Recalling the softness of Jo's lips and the way she'd surrendered in her arms, Lee was lucky to be standing at all. She'd explained that she needed to shower, change, grab some clothes, and contact Gary for an update, but that was only the partial truth. She really needed to remove herself from the situation and get a grip on her emotional state. Blaming her roller-coaster feelings on PTSD would have been the simple way out, but it was a weak argument at best.

She was wearing a hole through her rug thinking about what the UNSUB would do when Tory didn't show up tonight. Gary's profiler suggested that Tory's refusal to show could quite possibly push him over the edge, meaning Jo would be thrust into danger, and there was no way to know when or where it would come from.

She had decided to stay the night in one of the many guest rooms to be nearby if the stalker tried something, so she placed her clothes in a carry-on. No way could she let Jo out of her sight right now. Not after everything that had happened.

The FBI had done its own profile on the stalker and had termed him as an "intimacy-seeking stalker." People that fit that profile weren't likely to disappear and believed that they were loved, or would be loved, by the victim they stalked, if only they could get their attention. They normally focused on someone of higher-class status, like celebrities, and more often than not were mentally ill and delusional. No big surprise there. The profile also suggested that the stalker might suffer from a narcissistic personality disorder and possess low self-esteem. All this meant was that Gary's profiler had been correct from the start. Tory's plan to ignore his love for her would make him become more unpredictable, more violent.

Lee read the profile numerous times to commit it to memory. Words such as *loner* and *highly intelligent* stood out, and as she was about to leave and rejoin Jo at the house, the phone rang, making her jump. "Winters."

"Hi."

Lee closed her eyes, her hands trembling. Jo's voice held the power to turn her to mush, and she was glad for the momentary distance. "Hey, yourself. Need something before I come back?"

"Just you. I wanted to make sure you were coming back."

The response made Lee's knees go weak. "I'll be there."

"Okay. See you then."

Given the lines she had crossed, it was inevitable that Lee felt her barriers, her carefully constructed defenses, beginning to fragment, ready to shatter at any moment. She had a decision to make. Should she break down completely and let Jo in? Or should she do the sensible thing and run? A relationship between them could never work, because even if the professional part of their relationship wasn't in place, it wouldn't be fair for Jo to have to deal with all of her emotional baggage. Jo would say she could, but when she saw the real damage and woke up to Lee's screaming nightmares, could she really endure being with someone so broken? No. It wasn't fair to expect that of her. When the stalker was behind bars and Jo was safe, she'd have to bow out of Jo's life for good.

She pocketed her keys and grabbed her bag, not looking forward to the stressful night ahead. She'd accepted loneliness long ago, but that didn't mean she had to like it.

❖

Jo glanced up as the large grandfather clock in the library struck four a.m. Lee sat near the window, a book in her hand she wasn't even pretending to read anymore. She couldn't possibly sleep, knowing that somewhere out there a man had waited for Tory to meet with him and realized a few hours ago she wasn't going to show up. Jo wished she could sleep in order to wipe away everything she'd read about stalkers on the Internet and about their psychotic behaviors. Out of all the information she'd acquired, one common theme hit her hard. Stalkers didn't normally change their behaviors and only tended to become more obsessive over time. If they couldn't stop themselves, they had to be stopped. That thought alone made her shiver. If they didn't catch him soon, how long would they have to live in fear?

"Cold?" Lee asked.

"Yes, thank you." Jo accepted the fleece blanket and placed it over her legs.

"You really should try to get some sleep. The house is locked tight and there's plenty of muscle staying the night."

"Yeah, right. I'm so amped I don't think elephant tranquilizers could help me sleep."

"Can I get you something then?"

Jo threaded her fingers through Lee's and yawned. "Just you being here is enough."

"Jo, be reasonable. It's late and I think it would be best if you turn in. You've had quite a day." Lee stifled the protest that was coming with a little shake of Jo's hand. "What I mean is…" She inched closer. "You look tired and I don't want you getting sick. You're still recovering."

"Are you saying that you care about me?" Jo asked, staring at Lee's lips.

"I think we've established that I do."

"And what do you plan to do about it?" Jo held her breath as Lee leaned forward, waiting in anticipation for those perfect, warm lips to touch hers when the phone on Lee's belt began to vibrate. *When am I going to catch a break?*

"Winters," Lee said, clearing her throat.

"Lee, I have something and it's important," Gary said.

"Go ahead."

"Not over the phone. Too many ears, if you know what I mean. How about we meet in an hour."

"Location?"

"Sand and sun."

"Roger that. See you then."

"Where are you going?" Jo asked, refusing to let go of Lee's hand as she stood.

"To meet with Gary. He has some information he doesn't want to share over the phone."

"You will be careful, right?"

"Worried about me, Ms. West?" Lee's voice showed a trace of humor.

"As a matter of fact," Jo wrapped her arms around Lee's waist, "I am. It would seriously piss me off if something happened to you, so I don't want any holes in this sexy body of yours. You got me, soldier?"

"Roger that." She pulled Jo close and wrapped her in a strong embrace. "I have to go."

"Will you be back later?"

"Yes." Lee kissed her soundly, reverently. "I promise."

❖

Lee straddled a stone bench directly outside the entrance to the popular state park. She had notified the FBI that she was going out so they knew to watch out for Jo, but she still wanted to get back as quickly as possible. The beach had closed shortly after sunset the night before and wouldn't open until sunrise, which made this particular meeting place perfect to discuss private matters. Gary arrived a few minutes later, surprising Lee by using crutches and wearing a prosthetic leg. He'd always said that he'd be damned if he'd ever wear a fake leg, but he'd never elaborated on why. Apparently something was changing for the better in Gary's life. He handed her a blank manila folder, his grim expression suggesting that the contents didn't bear good news.

She read the information carefully before looking out over the rhythmic ripples of water. Peace had descended over the early morning, but she'd learned from experience that it was always calm before the storm. "Who else knows about this?"

"As far as I know, just the FBI."

"And should I ask how you got this information so quickly?"

He shook his head. "Probably not wise."

A tinge of color lit the sky on the horizon. Dawn was breaking, and the new day marked more trouble for the West sisters. "This isn't going away, is it, Gary?"

"Afraid not, and I wish I had a different answer. This guy is resourceful, Lee. I mean...the chemicals he used in Franklin's death were common household shit. Anyone could have logged onto the Internet to put that bomb together. He wanted them to think he was an amateur, but a voice-recognition trigger? Jesus Christ."

"I feel ya, buddy. Give me your take?"

"Wow, this is a first," he said in surprise as Lee glared sideways at him. "You never ask for my opinion. But I think this guy used to be military and is more resourceful than we give him credit for. Someone called Amanda at home moments before the kitchen exploded, triggering the explosion and destroying everything within five hundred feet of the blast. It took ATF and the FBI until last night to find even a small piece of the device. They were lucky it wasn't completely destroyed and that a few of the serial numbers could be detected. He finally fucked up. At least we know something about him now."

She'd been thinking along the same lines since the killer used the word "shadow" in one of his letters. Gary's opinion confirmed her suspicions. "Tell me."

"For one, the military tested this type of equipment a few years back but decided at the last minute to scrap the project. My insiders told me that a few of these triggers went missing, but unless you knew what they were, you'd probably mistake them for a common light switch. Now you and I both know you can't walk down to the nearest Radio Shack and pick up that kind of shit. And they don't make them anymore because they were unreliable. As far as I could tell, the only way he could know about these triggers and get access to them was if he served."

"So you said *used* to be military? Not anymore?"

Gary nodded. My profiler is confident that the UNSUB has military experience but wouldn't be mentally fit to serve now. Yeah, the bastard can create a bomb but is twitchy and wouldn't do well under gunfire in his delicate state."

"The profiler actually used the word *twitchy?*"

"No." Gary laughed without humor. "He used some technical mumbo jumbo about PTSD and crap I didn't understand."

Now there was a topic she understood all too well. A fellow soldier suffering from the same disorder but unfortunately lost in his own psychosis. If he hadn't killed someone or gone after Jo, she might have actually felt sorry for him. "I think it's time we ask for outside help."

"Who you got in mind?"

"Teigs," she said. Gary didn't even try to hide his shock.

"Are you crazy?"

"Do I look like I am?"

"Okay, let me rephrase," he said at Lee's look. "Are you sure? Teigs is an A-1 wacko. Don't get me wrong. I know he was the best. In fact, I seem to recall that fucker could find dynamite in a six-foot hole in the middle of the Sahara. It was like his nose was a needle on a compass and explosives had a magnetic field pointing him north. But I remember what happened the last time you talked with him. I'm surprised you let him live."

"Just do it." She stood, checking her watch. The more time she spent away from Jo, the more her anxiety mounted. "He's our only chance because we're running out of options, and I have virtually no faith in the FBI. Let's just hope the crackpot we know can keep it together long enough to find the more dangerous crackpot."

CHAPTER EIGHTEEN

The man screamed obscenities, grabbing at his hair and pulling it out by its roots.

The empty mirror frame lay in tatters before him. He dropped to his knees, trying desperately to scoop up the shattered pieces. He pieced the mirror together meticulously, hoping the Angry Man would speak to him again. He was his only friend and he lowered his eyes in reverence, praying to hear the venomous voice.

"Pathetic."

"You're still talking to me?"

"But of course. You amuse me, little man. Who else would put up with you?"

"Why do you torture me?"

"Because I can."

The man sat and tipped his head back in exhaustion.

He needed to pull himself together before the Angry Man tore him mentally to pieces.

"I thought you were done with me? I thought you and that bitch...oh...wait..." He laughed. "She didn't show, did she?"

"No."

"What did I tell you? You failed—again." The man squared his shoulders defiantly.

He had heard enough. The time had come to put his next plan into action. He wouldn't be a failure any longer.

"What are you going to do now? You've already proved you can't live without me. Can you, little man?" The eyes looking at him were barren, shark's eyes in a black sea.

"No. But she will pay, just like all the rest."

"What do you mean all the rest?"

"Remember Ramadi?" he asked as he pushed angrily away from his desk. He remembered it well. He retrieved the picture from his pocket and smiled at the woman's face staring back at him. He rubbed it over his crotch, letting out a small moan. Gary had never been worthy of Tory's love, and after last night they would all pay for Tory not coming to their meeting. Gary. Jo. Lee. No one was safe. When it was all said and done, they would all die and Tory would finally be his.

"I remember."

"That's your answer."

CHAPTER NINETEEN

Lee arrived at one of the seedier apartment complexes located in downtown San Mateo, a halfway house of sorts
for people with all types of disabilities. Michael Teigs was one of
those people—highly unstable yet a genius in his trade. She'd never
liked or trusted Teigs, but she needed to put her personal feelings
aside if Jo was ever going to have a chance at a normal life.

She knocked on apartment door 212 and waited for Teigs to
answer. When he pulled open the door, he grunted in disgust.

"'Bout damn time, Winters," he said, returning to his seat in
front of a mass of wires and tools.

Teigs peered at her over the rim of his wire-framed glasses,
mumbling incoherently. He was thinner than she remembered, his
face gaunt, his eyes withdrawn. He'd been released from the army
due to physical injuries and PTSD, but his symptoms were quite
a bit more severe than Lee's. From the file Gary had dug up on
Teigs, not only did he not sleep well and have concentration issues,
he was also prone to irritability and anger. Anger that had morphed
into violence more than once.

Teigs had been a demolition expert the likes of which no one
had ever seen. But even Teigs had fallen victim to the war and had
his life's prospects ripped away, like so many of them had. What
was left was a haggard-looking individual with a receding hairline
and a faint tremor on his right side.

"Been a while, Teigs."

"Cut the shit, Winters. Gary tells me you need my help."

"That's right."

"Must be pretty hard up if you're coming to see me?"

He had no idea how much she hated having to rely on him, and if he made one more derogatory comment, she'd have to forgo his help. "Can you help us or not?"

A smirk stretched his thin lips. "Oh, I can help. But what's it worth to ya?"

One reason she hated dealing with Teigs was his interest in playing games. He'd always played them, but she'd always won. "What do you want?"

Teigs laughed, rolling his chair away from the table. "It's not what I want, but what I need."

"Are we talking money?"

"What else is there?" he growled.

When he glanced at her this time, his eyes rolled around in their sockets, reminding her of marbles scattering across the floor. Oh, yeah, he'd completely lost it. "How much?"

"Well, that depends."

"On?"

"On how much that bitch's life is worth to you."

Teigs didn't have time to react, and even if he wanted to, he didn't have the ability to match Lee's speed or strength. She grabbed him roughly by the head and slammed his face into the table while holding a forearm to the back of his neck.

"You want to rephrase that, you little pissant, before I put you out of your misery and do the world a favor?" She'd kill him for talking about Jo that way. Snapping his worthless neck would be quick and painless, but she had come for information and needed it yesterday. "Well?"

"Stop, stop," he gasped. She released him, allowing him to slump against the desk under his own power. He tried rubbing the back of his neck, but the mechanical devices that replaced his once-skillful hands wouldn't allow it. He held up the claw-like metal extensions defensively. "What do you wanna know?"

"I want to know about the device this asshole used. You have the information from Gary. Tell me." She wasn't willing to waste any more time with this disgrace of a human being.

Teigs grabbed his hair, tugging at it roughly as his body twitched under the pressure. His eyes turned wild, his gaze distant. This was one of the many reasons he'd been discharged from the service, that and the mechanical hands that were of no use in his field. "This guy is good. Very good," he murmured. "I don't have the answers you need, but give me some time. I'll find them."

Lee pulled a hundred-dollar bill from her jacket and threw it on the table. "If you hear anything, call me."

Teigs grunted a response but Lee was already gone.

❖

"Marilyn, have you talked with Josh Peterson regarding the details for the book signing? If you haven't, could you please call Frederick's Books and verify the time and date change so there are no misunderstandings?" Tory asked.

"Sure, Tory, but I thought you and the girls talked about canceling," Marilyn said as Jo sat by and listened in on their conversation. "Surely you can't think about attending a book signing after this maniac has done everything except explain to you in detail how and when he's going to attack again?"

Tory looked up from the papers in front of her and rubbed her eyes. She'd spent all morning in the recording studio, had a meeting with her publicist in an hour, and needed to meet the group later to discuss their plans for the upcoming tour. "We did, but the FBI said it should be okay. They plan to have a strong police presence, and with our bodyguards there shouldn't be any problems. It's a public place and a single room, so they think they can control everything that happens."

"Tory, are you sure? I met those agents. They seem more intent on catching this guy than making sure you and the girls are safe."

"Look, the last thing I want is to debate you on what I should and shouldn't be doing. Just do what I ask," Tory yelled in a rare show of emotion.

Marilyn exited without further comment as Jo got up from the sofa and sat next to Tory's desk. "Wanna talk about it?"

Tory moved quickly to kneel in front of Jo's chair and rested her head against Jo's knee. Jo pulled Tory's hand into her lap, comforted by her presence. They had all been on edge since last night, due to Tory declining to meet with the stalker. Tory's simple touch acted like a kind of security blanket. Jo rubbed her thumb along the back of Tory's hand, waiting for her to say something. Instead of voicing her fears, Tory did something Jo hadn't seen since she was twelve years old. She cried.

Jo had always been the emotional one in the family. Tory never allowed emotions to interfere with any part of her life because they messed with her priorities. Avoidance was one of Tory's defense mechanisms and was most likely the reason she'd had an easier time dealing with their parents' deaths and was able to walk away from her relationship with Gary so easily. Lately, Jo had seen a new side to her, a gentler side. She finally understood that Tory's personal and public lives didn't differ much. They were both façades.

"Feel better?" Jo handed Tory a tissue as the sobs diminished to a few sniffs.

"Much. How about you?"

"Me? I'm not the one yelling at people and crying in her sister's lap. Let's not worry about me and concentrate on you," Jo said, poking the tip of Tory's nose with her finger. "What's with all the hostility?"

Tory wiped a forearm across her face. "It's everything. I'm so tired and things are happening so fast. I feel responsible for Amanda's death. I worry about you. When is this all going to end?"

Jo stroked the hair at the base of Tory's neck, feeling the muscles under her fingers start to relax. "I don't know, but I trust Lee and Gary to fix all of this."

"Me too. And since you brought it up, you want to tell me what's going on with you and Lee?"

Jo was surprised that it had taken Tory so long to ask. Normally she would have told Tory to mind her own business, but this was the first time in a long time that Tory had looked beyond herself and not only noticed what was going on, but cared enough to ask about it. "It's complicated."

"I knew it! What's happened between you two?"

"Nothing, really." Jo blushed.

"You are so busted! Can I say something without you getting mad?"

"Okay." Jo tensed, bracing for one of Tory's what-the-hell-are-you-doing speeches.

"Relax. I was just wondering if you're sure this is a good idea? I mean, she *is* your bodyguard."

"It's my business, Tory," Jo said, her words holding a warning.

"Hey, I didn't mean to pry and it's obvious that she cares for you, but…well, how does she feel about all of it?"

Therein lay the million-dollar question. Jo would love to have the answer, but every time they talked, Lee slammed the door on anything personal. Her physical guard had come down, but her emotional guard was still intact. Tory placed two comforting hands on top of Jo's, which were balled into fists.

"Jo, hear me out. I was engaged to a soldier and I know how they operate. I remember the day Gary told me to go. He wouldn't explain why, but he said I needed to leave and move on because it was better for both of us. Those were his words, but his eyes were telling me something different. I felt hurt and betrayed because he kept secrets and wouldn't tell me how *he* was really feeling. Deep down, I knew he was hurting because the signs were all there, but I couldn't get him to open up."

"And what does that have to do with Lee?"

"Don't you see, sweetie? You're a mission to her right now, and getting involved with you sheds new light on her priorities. Who knows what's going through her head? That scar on her arm didn't come from a knitting class gone bad. If she's anything like Gary, there's a lot you don't know."

Jo hated what she was hearing but Tory was right. Lee's hesitancy, her refusal to talk about anything personal—if she was ever going to stop Lee from leaving, she'd have to find a way to get her to open up. "I don't want her to run from me but she won't tell me a thing. We haven't even…"

"Oh…You mean you and she…"

Jo shook her head.

"But the possibility's there? It is serious."

"I told you it's complicated."

Tory gave Jo's hand a little squeeze. "It always is."

Lee arrived at the West residence shortly after nine that morning. She was still straddling her bike, trying to shake off the dirty feeling she had after meeting with Teigs. She'd never trusted that asshole, and she tried to keep her foul mood in check as she answered her phone. "Winters."

"Whoa. Guess I don't have to ask how it went," Gary said.

"Nope."

"Well, what did he say?"

"I asked him a question, pushed his head into a table, then threatened him with bodily injury if his attitude didn't improve."

"Right." He chuckled. "I see nothing's changed."

"Actually, that's where you're wrong. Remember I told you one day I was going to kill that little prick?"

"How could I forget?"

"Well, when this is over, that will no longer only be a threat," Lee said, climbing off her bike. "If he so much as sneezes on me I'll break his scrawny neck. Anything new for me?"

"Nothing. All my sources are coming up empty. But I should have those results for you regarding the soil samples and plant residue found on the tires from the accident shortly."

"Damn it. I should have had those weeks ago, Gary. We're running out of time. That book signing is tomorrow and I don't think Teigs is going to give us shit! He's bat-shit crazy. Those soil samples may be our only link to this bastard."

"I know, but this stuff takes time, and I agree with you about Teigs. Don't worry. I'm on it and I have some other leads cooking. Are you at the residence yet?"

"Just arrived."

"Okay. Call you at 1400."

Lee entered Tory's study to find Jo sitting in a chair with Tory's head in her lap. From the tired looks on both their faces, their day was turning out to be even tougher than hers. "Sorry. Didn't mean to interrupt."

"No, that's okay," Tory said, rising wearily. "I was leaving anyway."

"Really, ma'am, that's okay. I can just wait—"

"Lee. Stay," Tory said firmly. She squeezed Jo's hand. "Remember what I said, Sis."

Jo nodded but kept her eyes fixed on Lee as she sat across from her, their knees slightly touching.

"Did you get some sleep?" Lee asked, looking at the dark circles under Jo's eyes.

"Sleep?" Jo said. "Yep, that's exactly what I did. Since you left at four a.m., I took a hot bath, had some tea, and slept like a baby while you were out meeting Gary about some crazed lunatic wanting to kill me and do God knows what with my sister. Did I mention he's already killed one of Tory's bodyguards and injured me to make a point?"

"Point taken." Lee raised her hands in defense. "I fold."

Jo's body visibly relaxed and she smiled slightly. "You shouldn't have played in the first place."

"Maybe you're right."

"Maybe?"

"You know, Ms. West, we could have used your interrogation services in the military," Lee said hoarsely as Jo's thumbs rubbed firmly against the inseams of her jeans. Just a few inches higher and she might very well embarrass herself.

"Ha! Could you see me in the military? Taking orders, no less."

"No." Lee leaned forward so that their lips were a fraction apart. "But they definitely missed out."

"Their loss."

Lee's hands trembled where they rested on her thighs. Her pulse quickened as she closed the small distance between them and touched her lips to Jo's. The kiss was feather light and became more insistent as her tongue sought entrance. The moment was one of pleasure and pain, pleasure so intense she ached for it to continue but a pain so deep it forced her to back away. She would have sacrificed everything for one more kiss, but somewhere a man still threatened to do Jo harm. "I need to get back to work," Lee said breathlessly.

"No, please, don't leave." Jo held Lee's hands tight.

Lee didn't hear "don't leave." What she heard was, don't leave *me*. She pulled Jo against her and held her close, stroking her hair. If Jo needed her close, that's where she would be.

CHAPTER TWENTY

Josh Petersen, the store manager for Frederick's Books, waited while the five remaining employees put the finishing touches on the decorations welcoming Total Femme and their fans. The book signing was due to take place tomorrow afternoon, and the crew had worked tirelessly all evening to make sure every detail was covered.

"Good night, Josh."

"Night, Marty," Josh said, preparing to lock the door.

"Excuse me." Someone tapped Josh on the shoulder from behind.

"May I help you, sir?"

"Can I use your restroom?" the man asked, holding his groin like he was in pain. "Don't think I can hold it."

"Of course," Josh said, reopening the door. "If you need the handicapped bathroom, it's to your left."

The man grumbled a thank you and returned a few minutes later smiling in obvious relief. "Thanks. Sorry to hold you up."

"No problem at all."

"Something big happening tomorrow?" the man asked, eyeing the streamers and banners.

"You could say that. Total Femme's coming to sign their new book."

"Total Femme? What's that? Some kind of band?"

"Yep." Josh laughed. "Something like that."

"Well, whoever they are, the place looks great."

"Thanks," Josh said, slipping the keys into his pocket. "Anything else I can do for you?" he asked as the man stared intently at the interior of the bookstore.

"No, but thanks." The man patted Josh awkwardly on the shoulder. "You've already helped enough."

❖

Jo retired early and decided to take a bath and immerse herself in a good book in an attempt to get her mind off the book signing. She'd never understand how someone like Lee could do the job she did. Staring at the store's blueprints all day, talking incessantly about where they were going to stand, where each member was going to sit, how many people were allowed inside at any given time, and so on. She'd been bored to tears within the first hour, and the stress emanating from Tory's office could be felt within a ten-mile radius. Closing her bedroom door had been like erecting an imaginary force field, shielding her from all the crap in her life. She was tired and stressed, and, most of all, she missed being Lee's only focus.

At first, having all that attention directed at her had been annoying. She hated feeling like a specimen squirming under a microscope with someone analyzing her life piece by piece. But after a while, she'd wanted Lee to look at her. She'd gone out of her way to wear clothes that were a tad more revealing. She'd craved Lee's reaction to that midnight-blue dress and had only purchased it because Lee said she was beautiful in it.

Today, though, Lee's military expertise was in full force. Jo had sat in that room watching her in action and had to admit, it was quite a turn-on. Lee wasn't only a take-charge individual but was also the person all the other bodyguards respected and turned to for orders. She had no idea what terror Lee had witnessed in distant lands, but it was clear that she'd always been in charge and that soldiers under her command would follow her into the pits of hell and never ask why.

With Lee's focus on more urgent matters, Jo had focused on herself. Becoming more mobile had become her number-one priority, and within the last week she'd managed to move around comfortably without the cane. She still needed the brace when she stood for extended periods of time, but she was satisfied with her progress and in a few weeks hoped she wouldn't need it.

Her thoughts traveled back to Lee and she inhaled sharply. So much was still left unsaid between them. Lee's barriers had come crashing down one by one since the first time they kissed, but lately, some kind of new barrier had been erected. Lee would touch her but with a distance in that touch. Every brief caress felt as though it were their last. Every time she looked in Lee's eyes she saw pain and regret. She'd been thinking a lot about her last conversation with Tory. Lee wasn't only contemplating leaving. If Jo didn't find a way to obliterate some of those barriers, Lee's leaving was inevitable.

"Come in."

Lee took one step into Jo's bedroom and stopped as if she'd hit a brick wall. Though it could have been because she forgot what she was going to say, Jo figured it was more likely due to the sheer black negligee that left very little to the imagination.

"Do you like it?" Jo asked, pleased with Lee's reaction. She'd been saving it for a special occasion and hoped she'd be able to model it for Lee. If the crimson color in Lee's cheeks was any indication, she'd chosen wisely. Part of her had hoped Lee would visit her before settling in for the night.

"Uh…"

"*Uh* is not an answer."

"It's…yes…" Lee shook her head as if trying to focus. Sweat broke out above her brow. "I should…go."

Jo slid out of bed and slowly walked to Lee. The negligee clung to her like a second skin and her nipples stood out like two hard stones under the thin material. "Go? You just got here." She touched Lee's flushed face just before Lee pulled her forcefully into her arms. Lee buried her face between Jo's neck and shoulder. One of them groaned, but Jo wasn't sure which of them it was.

"Jo," Lee whispered.

She pulled back in Lee's arms and looked into her troubled eyes. "Oh, God. What's hurting you, baby?"

The pain and frustration on Lee's face tore at Jo's heart. Clearly Lee was struggling with her feelings, although she wasn't completely sure why.

"Come here." Jo guided Lee onto the bed beside her.

"This isn't a good idea."

"Shh…no arguing. Close your eyes."

"You want me to close my eyes while I'm in bed with you and you're half naked. Jesus, I'm only human."

"I like the way you think and there will be time for that later. I promise. But right now, I want to hold you."

They crawled into bed and slid under the covers. Jo snuggled against Lee and they lay there quietly, neither saying anything for a long time.

A wisp of time had passed when Lee opened her eyes and realized she had dozed off. Jo had drawn the shades so the soft glow of the bedside lamp was the only light in the room. Jo tenderly stroked her abdomen in soft, idle circles. Lee had no idea if Jo's actions were to relax or excite, but the twitch in her abdomen said her libido was gearing toward the latter.

"How long was I out?"

"About an hour. I guess you needed it."

There hadn't been a time in the past year, hell, in the past ten years, where she had slept so peacefully. No dreams, no demons to haunt her sleep. Jo's magical touch seemed to have stroked them away, creating light where there had only been darkness. "An hour? Damn. I need to get back."

"Back to what? It's late and everyone's gone for the night."

"I just have to go. I'm sorry."

"Sorry." Jo sat up. "Why are you always sorry when we spend time together?"

Lee stood, needing distance to think. She couldn't think when Jo touched her, especially wearing something so sheer that showed off her utterly stunning body, and lately her thoughts were becoming even more muddled than before she'd accepted the job as Jo's bodyguard. This concerned her because she didn't know how much longer she'd be effective at protecting Jo without risking her safety. The thought simultaneously sickened and saddened her. "Because we shouldn't…I shouldn't be here, Jo."

"Why? We're two adults. How can you deny what you feel for me?"

Lee lowered her eyes. "Because you're not safe with me."

"That's ridiculous. You're my bodyguard. I'm safer with you than anyone."

"You think that, but you don't know me, what I'm capable of."

"I do know you," Jo said, going to her. She wrapped her arms around Lee's waist and laid her head against her chest. "I've never been safer with anyone. I trust you."

"You shouldn't. I'm…broken." Lee backed away and ran a trembling hand through her hair. "I'll see you tomorrow."

Lee ran down the stairs, not wanting to explain further. Hiding behind her responsibilities wasn't going to work any longer, and keeping her distance was the only way to make sure that nothing happened between them. Another few minutes in that room and she would have forgotten all about her pledge to keep Jo safe. Her constant hunger for Jo was ripping at the last of her restraint, and if she didn't keep a safe distance, her hunger would eventually conquer her control and she'd devour Jo without mercy.

She ran into Dan Powers at the bottom of the stairs, and he explained some last-minute changes by Tory regarding the next day's events. At least this time she'd been prepared for any eventuality. "Anything else, Dan?" she asked tiredly.

"Nothing for now. Let's just hope these are the only surprises we have tomorrow."

Lee nodded, hoping for the same.

CHAPTER TWENTY-ONE

Lee was used to awaking most mornings feeling edgy and disconcerted, but today the feelings were magnified tenfold. Nothing had seemed quite right since she'd opened her eyes at five a.m., after tossing and turning all night, drifting frequently between consciousness and sleep. She had meticulously reviewed every detail regarding the book signing, from the time the entourage would leave the West home until the time they were to return. She'd even taken the time to do a walk-through the day before, making sure she was happy with the final arrangements and, more important, that she'd be able to remove Jo if they needed a quick escape. There would be a two-hour window from the time the group arrived until the time they would be safely back inside the limos. Two hours was a hell of a lot of time to give a determined crazy man.

She showered and changed quickly in one of the guest bathrooms on the first level of the West home. She refused to leave the house until the UNSUB was caught, not wanting to be far away from Jo if the UNSUB tried to make a move. But sleeping in the same house, knowing Jo was wearing that little black nightie, was damn near impossible. So close, but so far. She grabbed a bite to eat and was about to go see if Jo was awake, but before she did that she needed to call Gary for a quick update. She stepped outside into the cool morning air. With every unanswered ring, her agitation intensified.

"You rang?" Gary asked, towering over her from behind. She still wasn't used to him being taller than her again.

"Why didn't you answer?" Lee said, slamming the phone shut hard enough to make Gary jump.

"Why would I when I'm standing in front of you?"

Sarcasm was going to get him killed and he didn't even know it. Besides being edgy, she was pissed off that she'd allowed Gary to sneak up on her. Damn. If she couldn't detect a six-foot-four guy approaching with one steel foot, how the hell was she going to protect Jo if something went wrong? "I can *see* that. Why are you here?"

"I called to talk with Tory this morning and she invited me." The slight blush on his cheeks told her there'd been more to their conversation. "Jo's friend Emily can't make it so there's an extra seat in Tory's limo."

"I see." Lee swore silently, wondering how many more surprises she was in for today.

"Hey. I can leave if you think I'll be in the way."

"No, it's okay. You know last-minute changes irk me. Is everyone else coming out or are we going in?"

"They'll be out in a sec."

Lee heard their voices before Jo emerged, followed by Tory and two of the other members of the band. Each member was flanked closely by their bodyguards and had their own limo waiting, all big enough for friends and family members attending. One particular person stood out from the rest and Lee clenched her fists, her jaw aching from gritting her teeth. Her head started to throb painfully.

"Hey," Gary asked cautiously. "Everything okay?"

"Fine," she growled, her eyes locked on Chance Dillingham. But it wasn't the stocky blonde bass player that caused her blood pressure to reach deadly levels. It was the taller blonde with the short spiked hair and piercing green eyes that caused her to consider very evil actions, especially since she was currently holding the door open for Jo.

Jo threw her head back and laughed when Charlene Avery whispered something into her ear. The hair on the back of Lee's neck stood at attention, and if she were an animal she would have bared her fangs. The thought that Jo might have turned to Charlene after Lee had pushed her away yet again made her feel like she was going to vomit. She had known various friends were staying in the house and attending the signing, but Charlene hadn't been on the list. If she had, Lee would have slept on the floor outside Jo's room all night. She pictured the black negligee and wanted to rip Charlene's head from her shoulders. Fuck it. If Jo wanted to flirt with Charlene that was fine with her, but other arrangements would have to be made for Lee's travel plans to and from the bookstore. No way would she be able to ride in a limousine confined with the both of them, touching and giggling. She'd rather face a firing squad.

Luckily Charlene disappeared into the back of Chance's limo instead of Tory's. Everyone exchanged pleasantries as she sat quietly across from Jo and kept her eyes glued to the passing scenery. She didn't have to look at Jo to know she was watching her. Jo had a way of stripping her bare, exposing her in ways she couldn't explain. She couldn't chance losing her resolve now, not with so much on the line. Focus was the key for the next few hours. Distractions were inexcusable, especially when the price could be deadly.

A large crowd of fans had gathered excitedly outside the entrance to the popular bookstore, waving books and pens in the band members' direction. They'd been waiting anxiously for Tory, Chance, and Patricia to arrive after screaming wildly for the other band members, Darian Cross and Cynthia Evans, who had arrived only moments before.

Lee exited the vehicle first and held the door open for Tory and the others to emerge from the black stretch limo. She automatically scanned the area, looking for anyone or anything out of place. Tory got out first, and her bodyguards paved their way into the three-story bookstore. Lee assisted Gary with his crutches before offering her hand to Jo.

"This is crazy," Jo said right before someone rammed into her, causing her to stumble and lose her balance.

"Shit!" Without thinking, Lee lifted Jo off her feet and into her arms, maneuvered her carefully through the crowd, and set her down once they reached the safety of the bookstore.

"Why the hell did you do that?"

Lee adjusted her earpiece, listening to the chatter of the other bodyguards as they dropped into position. "Do what?"

"Do what? Are you serious? Pick me up, that's what."

"I didn't want you to get hurt." The simple statement appeared to have calmed the storm brewing in Jo's turbulent blue eyes. Lee glanced away from Jo and scanned the crowd, her jaw aching from it being locked tight.

"I'm sorry I snapped at you," Jo said, placing her hand on Lee's tense forearm. "Thanks for taking care of me."

"No need to thank me, Ms. West. It's what you pay me for."

Jo stepped back as if slapped, her anger resurging. "No, my sister pays you. I didn't want your help in the first place!"

Lee followed Jo as she moved to Tory's table and sat in the far corner. She stood directly behind her, rubbing her forehead in frustration. She hadn't meant to piss Jo off with her comment, but she'd worry about that later. Suddenly a voice she didn't recognize yelled out Jo's name and she moved to her, hovering above Jo in a protective stance.

"I don't get it," Jo said, clearly confused. "Why are they yelling for me? I'm no one."

Lee focused on the dozens of faces quickly gathering inside the room and said the first thing that came to mind. "Probably because you're beautiful."

"Excuse me?"

"Hey, you two," Gary said, saving Lee from a very embarrassing moment. "This is great, isn't it?" His eyes, like Lee's, continually scanned the crowd, and the lines around them belied his statement.

"Yeah, great," Lee mumbled, thankful for his interruption. Jesus! What was she thinking? This was the last straw. The time had come to admit that she could no longer control her emotions around Jo. If Gary hadn't made his not-so-subtle arrival, she could have exposed Jo to further danger.

Besides, what would the people who respected her think if they saw her in an intimate moment with Jolene West in public, especially when her job to protect Jo was supposed to be her number-one priority? What if in that moment, the stalker had decided to attack? Granted, it wasn't like she'd started stripping off her clothes or bent Jo over the table, but she'd allowed her concentration to waver, and that was more than enough. She could no longer deny she wanted to lose control with Jo—to be beside her, underneath her. She wanted to claim Jo—to be in her, on her. She constantly fought the urge to stroke Jo's cheek, to caress the skin that felt like satin under her touch. She yearned to drown in those blue pools that had the power to force the oxygen from her lungs with one simple look. She wanted to close the gap between them, to kiss the lips that were softer than the finest silk. Jo was beautiful, smart, funny, caring. She had it all, and Lee wanted it.

She focused on Josh Petersen, who was introducing himself to each of the band members. Tory sat behind a large stack of books and cast a smile in Jo's direction.

"Are we ready, everyone?" Josh asked excitedly, right before he opened the doors to admit the first wave of fans.

The first hour was uneventful as each band member signed books and chatted with excited fans. Next to Tory, Patricia Simpson had quite a following, but the three other members kept busy too. All the band members were clad in their usual leather garb, the new mesh tops that Patricia and Tory had found revolting giving tantalizing glimpses of the skin beneath. All five women were gorgeous, but Lee thought none of them compared to Jo.

"What do you think?" Gary stood next to her.

"I think I wanna get out of here."

"Me too. Seems quiet but…"

Lee looked up at Gary who was staring intently out the window. "See something?"

"Yeah. Outside, two o'clock."

Lee saw him immediately. A tall, lanky figure with a hood over his head was standing directly outside the window peering in through the tinted glass. She couldn't see his face, and it wasn't the sweatshirt in the eighty-degree heat that caused her to become hyper alert.

She followed his gaze, recognizing an object that hadn't been in the room during her last inspection. The microphone sitting on Tory's table wasn't supposed to be there. Josh picked it up and the hooded man stepped away from the window.

Lee lunged for Jo. "Get down!"

CHAPTER TWENTY-TWO

The room exploded in dust and smoke. Lee covered Jo with her body and people began to scream as debris rained down on them, a plume of gray ash blanketing what remained of the first floor, the smell of burning books acrid and dense. The familiar sounds of agony and looming death quickly filled the room. She felt as if she were reliving a nightmare until the echoes of horror that were present, not past, awakened her from the fog of old terror.

Coughing helped expel the Sheetrock dust from her lungs as she shook off the debris that had pinned her to the floor. She waited and exhaled in relief when she felt Jo move under her. *Thank Christ.*

"Are you hurt?" Lee asked, trying to shield Jo from the pandemonium around them.

"No." Jo coughed. "Are you?"

"I'm fine." Lee held her tight. "Oh, baby, I was so scared. I thought…" Lee's vision wavered and suddenly she found it hard to breathe.

"You thought…" Jo asked right before Lee slumped into her arms. "Lee? Lee!"

Jo cradled Lee in her arms and suddenly felt a sticky substance coating her chest and stomach. Glancing down, she saw the pool of blood that had soaked the left side of Lee's body. "Oh, my God, no!"

Jo screamed for someone to help, stroking Lee's sweat-soaked face. As the dust began to clear, she could make out two large forms coming closer. Thankfully it was Dan Powers and Ted Simons, clearing a path to get to them. "Dan, help me. She's hurt!"

Dan tossed aside a few pieces of broken ceiling tiles and crouched down next to them. "We need to get you out of here, Ms. West," he said, coughing into his hand.

"Where's my sister?"

"Safe. Everyone's safe. Now, please, let's go. We'll come back for her once you're secure."

"And leave her *here*?" *Had he lost his mind?* "Screw that!"

"Ms. West, look—"

"No, you *look*. Where she goes, I go. Discussion over." Throughout Lee's whole life people had abandoned her. First her parents, then the people she served with, though not by choice. Jo refused to be one of them.

"Okay. Ready, Ted," Dan said as he hooked his arms through Lee's and Simons grabbed both her feet. "On three."

They carried Lee out to the limousine that sat idling in the alley behind the building. Jo slid into the backseat and cradled Lee's head in her lap. She remained silent as they sped toward the hospital.

"Sweetie, are you all right?" Tory asked, squeezing in on the other side of Jo to hug her.

"Yes, you?"

"Fine. Some bumps and bruises but otherwise I'll survive. All the girls are safe too. I'm not sure about anyone else." Tory placed Jo at arm's length and gave her the once-over. "Jesus, you're covered in blood. Are you sure you're all right?"

Jo nodded but couldn't speak because of the lump in her throat. If Lee wasn't okay, she'd never be all right again. She motioned at Lee, and Tory gulped at the sight of the blood seeping from her left side.

"Hey, hey, come on," Tory said. "She'll be okay. Isn't that right, Gary?"

"Yep." He nodded, holding Tory's hand tight without looking away from Lee's inert form. "She's tough."

Jo stroked Lee's hair as Dan and Ted kept pressure on her injuries. As soon as they arrived at the hospital, Lee was wheeled into the emergency room and Jo sat helplessly waiting to hear about her condition.

"What am I going to do if something happens to her," Jo said to nobody in particular.

"Honey," Tory reached for her hand. "It's going to be okay. Lee is as tough as they come. She survived the desert, she'll survive this."

She slung an arm around Jo's shoulders but appeared surprised when Jo shrugged it off. Jo wasn't seeking comfort. She was so angry. She wanted someone to pay for hurting Lee—to suffer as much as she was suffering. Unfortunately, as years of built-up resentment finally bubbled over from a combination of frustration, anger, and fear, Tory was the unlucky one in her path. "We could have avoided this, avoided more injury and destruction. But oh, no. Tory West had to get her way again. Why was this damn book signing so important to you?"

"Because," Tory said calmly, "hiding from this maniac wasn't the right course of action."

"Right course of action?" Jo looked at Tory like she'd grown a second head. "Okay, you need to stop hanging around Gary. He's got you talking like a shadow now. Who cares whether it was right or wrong? The point is, you shouldn't have done it. You were warned but still you didn't listen."

"The FBI said it was fine. And what else would you have me do, Jo?" Tory said, sounding as defeated as Jo felt.

"Be more serious about protecting yourself. You want me under guard twenty-four seven, but you're the one this lunatic is really after, and still you do stuff like today to put yourself and others at risk. All I ever wanted was my sister back, Tory. The rest of it can go to hell."

"I'm here," Tory said, squeezing her hand. "I'm right here."

"For now, or at least until the next tour." Jo sighed. Suddenly she felt as if the life were sucked from her body and she sank into her chair. "I don't want to talk any more. I need to find out how Lee is."

"I know, but we can't leave things like this."

"Yes, we can and we will…for now. Just this once, you're not getting your way."

Tory took the hint that Jo wanted to be left alone and exited through the double doors, followed by her bodyguards and leaving Jo with one guard in the waiting room. Several hours had ticked by when a tall, attractive surgeon with dark hair and even darker eyes awakened her. Jo tried to stand but the doctor placed a comforting hand on her shoulders, stopping her from rising.

"I'm Doctor Ammini, Lee's surgeon," she said, extending her hand. "And you are?"

"Jo. How is she? Is she going to be all right? Did you—"

"Whoa, calm down—first things first. Are you Lee's family?"

"Yes," Jo lied. "Can I see her?"

"That depends."

"On?"

"On whether she wants to see you."

"Why wouldn't she want to see me?"

The doctor ignored her question. "The surgery went well but she's still groggy. When she woke a few minutes ago, she said no visitors. But," Doctor Ammini held up her hand as if warding off the next question, "I can ask if she can make an exception."

"She's awake?" Jo said as tears welled in her eyes.

"Yes. But, she's been through a lot today. Five minutes, okay?"

Dr. Ammini explained that Lee had lost a lot of blood from the injury sustained to her arm and side when a sharp ceiling tile had sliced her open and would be weak for the next few weeks until her blood counts rose. She would make a full recovery, but it would be slow. Somehow she'd also broken her arm, most likely when she'd tackled Jo to the floor. Jo stood in the doorway of Lee's room, content to watch her sleep peacefully. Sleeping, not dead. *Thank God.*

"You just going to stand there staring or are you coming in?" Lee asked weakly.

"I'm coming in," Jo said, her voice hoarse with anxiety. She searched for Lee's hand under the covers, surprised at the strength that squeezed back.

"I'm okay."

Jo laughed softly, ignoring the tears coursing down her face. "If you were okay, you wouldn't be in here."

"Ow, shit, that hurts!" Lee said as she tried unsuccessfully to move her left arm.

"Stay still."

"What about my arm?"

Jo ran her fingertips carefully over the injured limb. Thick, dark blotches were seeping through the heavily bandaged arm. "It's fine. A broken bone and some stitches but the doc says full recovery."

"So, I get to keep it?"

Jo didn't understand the question until she realized that Lee might not know where they were or what accident they'd been referring to. Doctor Ammini said they'd given Lee morphine and that she'd be pretty drugged up for the next few days. "Yes," she said, choked up. "You get to keep it."

"That's good. I'm tired—so tired," Lee said, her eyes closed and the worry lines in her face relaxing.

"Rest. I'll be here."

"Yeah?"

Jo placed a kiss on her forehead. "Try to get rid of me."

CHAPTER TWENTY-THREE

L ee felt sluggish and out of sorts. She couldn't raise her left arm. Was she dreaming again? Trying to sit up, she groaned as the pain forced her to fall back into the pillows. *I'm in a hospital. Shit, not again!* She looked at the needle in her arm and followed the tube to the bag hanging next to the bed. Morphine. She groaned.

The strong narcotic always caused her to hallucinate, and what infuriated her most was that it rendered her helpless by making her lose touch with her body. She hated being out of control and tried fighting the effects, but the strong hold the drug had on her nervous system left her loose-limbed, like a marionette without a puppeteer.

A headache and nausea always followed the haziness. She had no idea how long she'd been out, but judging from the telltale signs of the sun illuminating the drab hospital room, it had at least been overnight. Frustration rippled through her. The morphine wasn't allowing her to think clearly. There was someone she needed to find, someone who needed her. She had to get to her. Reaching for the IV, she was about to rip it out of her arm when she noticed a mass of long blond hair sprawled across her covered legs. A snore emanated from under the hair and she was thankful the motion hadn't woken Jo, who was a sound sleeper.

Sifting the long blond strands through her fingers, she was suddenly content to lie there watching Jo sleep. This was the someone she needed. She would've given anything to stay like that forever, but the slow, steady beat behind her eyeballs suddenly increased, making her wince in pain. Her loud groan made Jo stir and wake up.

"Hey."

"Hey."

Jo sat up, stretching the kinks out of her back and neck. "What time is it?"

"Time for you to go home and get some rest."

"Nice try," Jo said, wiping a sweat soaked strand of hair out of Lee's eyes. "But I'm not leaving until you do. How do you feel?"

"How do I look?"

"Your eyes are hazy and a little red. Morphine making you a bit loopy?"

"Yeah," Lee admitted reluctantly. "I hate the stuff."

"I'll talk to the nurse about lowering the dosage. How about the rest of you?"

"Confused. Sore. I don't remember much."

"We'll talk later."

"That'll work, but I have to go to the bathroom, and that can't wait until later."

"Let me help you."

"No, I got it." Lee tried to move but a bolt of pain seared down her left side. She grimaced but refused to cry out again in front of Jo.

"You're unbelievable!" Jo said, reaching for her. "This is no time to be a stubborn, macho soldier. Now stay put and let me or the nurses help you."

Lee grimaced as nausea threatened with each breath. "You… should…go."

"I said I'm not going anywhere. Be quiet and hold on, or I'll make one of these scary-looking nurses come in and give you a sponge bath or something."

"That's a threat?"

"If you saw these nurses you'd think so." Jo grinned. "Come on. Be a good patient and put your arm around my shoulders."

"And you think I'm stubborn."

"Looks like we have something in common."

After returning from the restroom Jo helped Lee get settled back in the bed, and Lee felt like she'd run a hundred miles instead of just shuffling to the bathroom.

"Right. Go to sleep. I'll still be here when you wake up."

Lee nodded. "Is everyone okay? Tory and the others?"

Jo winced. "Two FBI agents were killed, the ones standing closest to Tory when the bomb went off. Some of the customers were hurt, but the band is fine. Thanks to you."

Relieved, Lee closed her eyes and slept well into the afternoon. Jo kept vigil by Lee's bed, watching over her as she slept.

❖

Lee woke to the familiar tangle of hair that covered her thigh just above the covers. She gently ran her hand through it, pushing away the strands that covered Jo's eyes. Below her hand Jo stirred, a small, incoherent grumble escaping her lips. She hadn't meant to wake her, but the need to touch her had been too great.

Lee felt defenseless against the pull of emotions that having Jo so close provoked. She'd never felt so helpless, so lost in another human being. Maybe it was the medication. But maybe it was because she simply didn't want to resist Jo any longer. She would allow herself this moment of comfort—a final minute that would be imprinted in her memory forever. Waking up to find someone there, someone who cared what happened to her, was comforting in a way she'd never experienced.

"Lee?"

"Yeah, wake up, sleepy." Lee's hand slipped off Jo's shoulder as she stirred. Jo's hair was tousled and her eyes hazy from sleep. *God, you're beautiful.* "You need to go home and get some rest."

"Told you." Jo yawned and stretched. "Not going anywhere."

"You have to. It's late and there's nothing you can do for me here."

More alert now, Jo twined her fingers with Lee's beneath the covers. "Let me be the judge of that. How do you feel?"

"Rough, but I'll manage."

"I'm sure you will." Jo smiled gently. "Actually, I'm glad you're awake. After what happened, I realize that we should have talked sooner. If something had happened to you…" Jo's voice broke.

"It didn't. I'm fine." It killed her to see Jo in so much pain.

"And I'm so glad. But I want to tell you—"

"No! Don't say it. Please." *I know what you're going to say. I can see it in your eyes. Can't you understand what those words would do to me? I can't protect you any longer. I love you so much, but I'm saving you from the demons that haunt my life and will eventually destroy you.*

"But it's true. I refuse to deny anymore that I love—"

"No! I said stop!" *God, don't make this harder for me.* She couldn't handle another punch to her heart. Why did Jo have to say that word? Damn it, why? Couldn't Jo understand this was her ultimate sacrifice, that her love could destroy Jo, destroy them both?

"I don't understand. Why are you doing this?" Jo stared at her, pain clouding her eyes.

"Because I don't feel the same way." Lee looked away, feeling as though her heart were being ripped from her chest. She couldn't lie to Jo while looking her in the eyes. "I care for you." She swallowed hard, knowing the next words she spoke would deliver the final blow. "But my feelings stem from my job, a job I no longer can do effectively. I'm sorry if I misled you in any way."

Jo's jaw tightened, her blues eyes glacial. "Don't beat yourself up," Jo said angrily, and moved to the door. She turned and pinned Lee with a hard stare. "I thought you were a lot of things, but I never took you for a coward."

The second the door slammed behind Jo, a new ache began in the center of Lee's chest—a pain no amount of morphine could mask. With every burning inhalation she tried to convince herself that her decision had been for the best. Her tears fell silently as she lay alone in a bed of her own making.

❖

Lee checked out of the hospital the following day, not wanting to risk Jo returning while she sat numbly inside her medical prison.

Not an hour, hell, not even a minute, had gone by since she'd sent Jo away that Lee hadn't thought about her. Jo's radiant smile and intense blue eyes haunted her. The hours that had passed had been filled with pain—physical and emotional. She deserved to suffer, just like she'd suffered when everyone under her command had lost their life, while she had escaped with just an arm injury. Losing her men had nearly taken her sanity, and now losing Jo cut deeper than any knife and created a void deeper than any bullet. It left splinters imbedded under her skin that no instrument could remove. It hurt to take a breath, to take a step.

She'd called Gary when she was released from the hospital, and when he came to get her he confirmed what Jo had told her: two FBI agents had been killed in the blast, and a number of civilians had been wounded. The suspicious person outside the window hadn't been identified. The exterior cameras had been destroyed in the blast, and no one except Gary and Lee had seen the man in the hoodie to identify him. It killed her to be away from Jo, but even if she'd wanted to go back, her injuries would make guarding Jo nearly impossible. Instead, she'd instructed Gary to double Jo's security, even though she knew Jo wouldn't approve. At this point she didn't care. If she couldn't be there, she'd have Gary build a wall of protection around Jo, anything to keep her from being harmed.

Gary drove her home and said, "If you want to talk, I'm here." Except for updates every few hours from him, she wouldn't say much. For the first time, she found the silence in the shadows deafening.

❖

Jo sat curled up inside the library, dabbing at her eyes with a tissue. Over a week had passed since she'd walked out of that hospital, a week since she'd talked to Lee and touched her in any way. She had no idea why Lee was refusing to admit that she had feelings for her. Should she call her and get her to understand that they were both suffering? But what would she say? Even though it killed her not to be able to take care of Lee, she refused to beg. The possibility of being rejected again was the only thing keeping her from picking up the phone instead of staring at it for hours on end.

"Jo?" Tory asked, leaning up against the doorframe. "You can't keep doing this to yourself."

"Go away."

"No. You need to talk to someone and I want to be here for you." Tory knelt in front of Jo and grasped her hand. "Say something. Anything. It's killing me to see you this way."

"I have nothing to say to you."

"Great, then I'll talk and you can listen. Let's start with how you told Lee you loved her and she turned you away." Tory smiled knowingly when Jo gasped. "And before you ask, I was in love with a soldier, remember? I know what you're feeling because I've been there."

"Talk about calling the kettle black," Jo said. "You're still in love with him."

"And how do you know that, smarty pants?"

"Because you never stopped. Go ahead, deny it. I dare you."

"I don't deny anything, but I was hoping this conversation would be about you. And yes, I do love him. I always have."

"But you're not with him?"

"No, I'm not," Tory sad sadly. "But remember what I told you about soldiers? They can't always express themselves without feeling weak."

Jo gasped, placing a trembling hand over her mouth. "I remember. I was so focused on the fact that she didn't want me…"

Oh, baby. I refused to hear what you weren't saying. "I need to talk with her! Call Gary and hand me the phone." She figured if Lee wouldn't talk with her she could always coax Gary into getting Lee to see her. If she couldn't reason with him, she'd have to find another way.

"Gary, I need to talk with Lee. Gone? What do you mean she's gone? Where the hell did she go?" Jo's voice rose. She was sick with worry. Lee had always been alone, and now she was injured somewhere with no one to help her. "Look, I know you're trying to be her friend, but what if she needs help? How could you leave her in the condition she was in? Damn it, what's wrong with you?" She hung up, no more the wiser after having called the only person in the world Lee was connected to.

Jo stared at her hands, feeling more helpless than at any other time in her life. "I need to see her."

"I know, honey. But maybe she needs time."

"How much time?"

"She's a soldier, Jo. Who knows?"

Jo nodded and laid her head on Tory's shoulder. She cried out her frustration with the entire situation. For now, it was all she could do.

Chapter Twenty-four

Jo went downstairs the next morning to find Tory sitting behind her desk with a look of terror on her face. "What is it? Another letter?"

"No, a phone call." Tory let her cell fall from her fingers and it clattered to the floor.

"What did he say? Did he hurt someone else?"

"No. He wants me and you to meet with him today—in an hour. Or else…"

"Jesus!" Jo grabbed Tory and shook her. "Did you tell someone? The FBI?"

"No!" Tory said nervously, looking into the hallway before closing her office door. She whispered, "We can't tell anyone. He knew the phones were bugged. That's why he called me on my cell."

"You're not making sense. We've already told everyone. Come on, Tory, you're scaring me. Spit it out already."

"He told me…" Tory swallowed hard. "He said that if anyone finds out, Gary and Lee will die."

"What!" Jo bolted for the door, only to be stopped by Tory. "Let me go!"

"Shh…calm down."

"Fuck that! He threatened Lee and she doesn't know. Damn it, Tory. We have to tell the FBI and stop this maniac."

"Jo, *listen* to me. We can't involve anyone. He said that if the authorities get tipped off, or if someone follows us, he'll detonate a bomb that he's placed at Lee's and Gary's home. We can't call them or contact them in any way. He said he'd know and that they'd pay if we disobey him."

The bile rose in Jo's throat. She had to get word to Lee, but she couldn't risk putting her in danger. *Think, damn it!* "I understand. So what do we have to do?"

"We're supposed to drive to an empty warehouse off the El Camino in San Mateo. From there we'll receive further instructions. He said we're to take the two-seater Porsche and make sure no one follows us."

Jo nodded but was only partially listening. She was already formulating a plan, but she wouldn't tell Tory. The less Tory knew the better, but if they were going to survive the rest of the day Lee would have to be notified. It was their only chance. She'd have to plan her timing so the stalker wouldn't know. "I'm in. What are you going to tell Dan and the other bodyguards?"

"We won't tell them anything. You and I are going to go outside and walk into the garage like we're just having a conversation. I'll tell the bodyguards to back off because we want privacy, and then we'll take the car before anyone notices. We'll take the service road off the property instead of leaving through the front gate."

"Damn, you've been hanging around Gary too long. Okay, it's a plan. Let's just hope it works. Meet you outside in five minutes."

She waited until Tory left her study before jotting down a quick note. She only hoped Dan or one of the other bodyguards was smart enough to look for it before it was too late.

For the third time in an hour, Lee reread the same article inside an old issue of *Guns and Ammo*. She hadn't left her apartment in days and felt more lost than before she'd been discharged from the army.

What she wouldn't pay to see Jo smile, to hear her laugh, to take back the words she'd forced herself to say so she wouldn't subject Jo to the misery that was her life. How she ached to tell Jo she loved her too, to take Jo into her arms and kiss the tears away that she'd caused. But as she looked around her bleak apartment, she wondered what someone like her had to offer to someone so full of life. Jo had many good years ahead of her. She was beautiful, strong, and so damn sexy. No, Lee wasn't the person for her. Jo deserved so much better than a washed-up ex-soldier, and she wasn't going to pretend otherwise.

Her arm was healing nicely, the pain more of a passing annoyance than anything else. The cast got in her way periodically, but she could live with it. She'd learned to deal with pain, to swallow her suffering like every good soldier was trained to do.

She threw the magazine on the table to deal with the insistent pounding on her door.

"Gary, what the hell?" Lee asked as he moved into her apartment, followed by Dan Powers and Ted Simons.

"Lee, he has them."

The roaring in Lee's head matched the ripping pain in her heart. A growl escaped her throat and, instinctively, all three men backed up. "What! How the fuck could you let this happen? Where's the FBI?"

"Hold on," Gary said. "We had no clue what was going on until Simons found this note addressed to you in Tory's study."

She ripped the note from Gary's hand and read it a half-dozen times. She forced her hands to remain steady as she held the only tie that bound her to Jo. If this maniac so much as touched a piece of hair on Jo's beautiful head, she'd rip him to pieces one body part at a time. "Did you find a bomb outside?"

"No," Dan said. "I had Simons sweep both our buildings before we made contact. Simons spent some time with an explosives expert in the service so he knew what to look for."

"Simons, how long were they gone before you found this letter?"

"Thirty minutes. We couldn't figure out why they left without protection, especially after the bookstore bomb, so I poked around the house and found this addressed to you. I know it's usually against regs to snoop, Sarge, but I didn't want to make any more assumptions."

Lee's lip quirked into a half smile, and for once in a long time she didn't mind that someone had called her by her former title. If it wasn't for his quick thinking, they would have lost a lot of valuable time. "Good thinking, soldier. Gary?"

"Yeah?"

"You have that report I asked you for last week?"

Gary nodded and reached into his satchel. Lee scanned the paperwork thoroughly, her eyes coming to life as a picture emerged. "I think I know where he's taken them."

"How do you know that?" Gary asked.

"Your profiler stated that the UNSUB would know everything about Tory, correct?"

"Yeah, why?"

"If that's the case, he would also know where she grew up. Look at these recent reports." She handed Gary back one of the sheets of paper. "Traces of a particular polymer were found that are only used in plastics made for the production of forts and tree houses. From the soil samples taken at the scene of Jo's accident and your report, it says here that adobe soil, Magnolia Virginiana and Baccharis Pitularis, are all commonly found in the Cordilleras Creek Area. Ring any bells?"

"Shit, why didn't I see that?" Gary said, hanging his head. "I failed her…again."

"No, you didn't. Without this, we wouldn't have any clue as to where they could be. Pull yourself together, soldier. I need that address now."

Gary straightened, her words penetrating his worry. "No problem, I already know it."

"Good. Dan and Simons, you come with me."

"Wait," Gary said. "Are we notifying our friends at the FBI?"

"No. Agent Steele couldn't find his dick in his pants. I'm not going to risk their lives again for that asshole's ego. We can handle this. We'll find this little fuck-head and make him regret breathing."

❖

Lee sat inside the black Expedition focused on what used to be the West sisters' original family home. No one in the car spoke. They were waiting for Gary to receive a phone call so Lee could gather the last piece of information she'd requested.

"Talk to me," she said, after he hung up his cell phone and scribbled a few things on a sheet of paper.

"I know who has them."

"Spit it out."

"Teigs. It was always Teigs." Gary's voice shook.

Could that be possible? Teigs was unstable and a nut, but even she didn't think he'd have the brains left or the means to pull something like this off. "Are you sure?"

"Positive."

"Give me the logistics."

He handed her a sheet of paper that contained an itemized list of what appeared to be common household cleaning agents. "This is the list of chemicals used in the bomb that killed Franklin. Ammonia…baking soda….basic bomb-making shit. This, though, is something else." He handed her the piece of paper he'd written on.

Lee stared at the piece of paper in disbelief. "PE-4?"

"Yeah, the good British stuff. Blows like C-4 but the velocity of detonation is quicker. Remember when Teigs worked with some of the British Special Forces on that project outside of Baghdad?

"I do. Some of that shit went missing."

"Exactly. But that's not all. Josh Petersen, the manager of Frederick's Books, woke from the coma he'd been in about an hour ago. He told that same friend of mine at the FBI that a skinny man wearing a hooded sweatshirt needed to use the restroom the night before. The microphone had been stored in the closet inside that restroom."

"So? That could have been a coincidence."

"Yes, but he also told them the man had two mechanical hands."

"Son of a bitch!"

"My sentiments exactly. So what's the plan?"

"Remember I told you what I would do to Teigs if I ever saw him again?" Lee said.

"I remember."

"It's time I make good on that promise.

CHAPTER TWENTY-FIVE

"Put the bitch in there." He pushed Tory and Jo into the familiar play structure they had spent many hours of enjoyment in as children.

Once he'd given them another set of instructions at the old warehouse, he'd waited until they had entered the dilapidated abandoned family home before he'd ambushed them. He'd hit Jo over the head with his gun and knocked her unconscious before ordering Tory to drag Jo's body to the rear of the house. Finally he had everything he'd ever wanted—the love of his life and a bonus—to kill the one person that would cause Lee Winters the greatest amount of pain.

"Please," Tory begged as she curled her body protectively over Jo's. "Leave her alone. I'm here—"

"Shut up!" Teigs snarled and grabbed Tory by the hair. He pulled her off Jo and threw her into a corner. "The only person you will love and protect from now on is me. Understand?" He kicked Jo in the ribs and received a quiet groan from her.

"No! Jo...please..."

"I said shut the fuck up!" He pointed his gun at Jo's head. "One more word and I'll put a bullet in her head."

He moved to the desk and placed his insurance policy in his pocket, the one item he would need if something went wrong. If that happened, he wouldn't be the only one to die.

"Look around you," he said. "I did all this for you."

Tory glanced around the room, her eyes wide with shock. Pictures of her were everywhere, on every inch of the walls and even a few on the ceiling, as well as articles of some of her greatest accomplishments. A Tory West shrine built out of his love for her. "But why?"

"Because I knew the first time I saw you, you'd be mine. You were on his arm but you didn't belong there. You belonged to me. Me!"

"What are you talking about? Whose arm…"

He hit her across the cheek with one of his mechanical arms, and she cried out in pain. An angry red welt instantly formed on her cheek, and blood ran from one of her nostrils.

"See what you made me do!" A growl tore from his throat as he swept all the wires and mechanical-looking devices on his table onto the floor. He gagged Tory, not wanting to hear anything from her until he was ready. "You must learn to obey me, love. I want you by my side like a good woman would be. And soon, I will show you exactly how a woman of mine should behave, especially when a man, like myself, treats you right." He ran his creepy metallic hand over his crotch and laughed when she shrank away. Suddenly he jerked his head toward the large broken mirror on the far wall.

"Now what?"

"I see you're losing your temper again, little man. She's yours. Why wait? Take her now!" The Angry Man stared past him at Tory.

Tory's whimper caught Teigs's attention and he turned to glare at her.

"She's as pathetic as you are," the Angry Man murmured, as Teigs turned back to stare at his reflection in the mirror.

"Don't talk about her that way," Teigs yelled. "Look at her. She's perfect."

"Actually, she is perfect. You were right, little man. But," he said, turning to stare intently at Jo, "I like her twin's sizzling personality better. The other one is too much of a whiner."

"It's another one of our differences. We've never seen eye to eye. Although, when I'm done, you can have her if you wish. My gift to you."

"Why…" The Angry Man in the mirror grinned. "Thank you, little man."

❖

Lee peered through the high-powered binoculars. A grayish van with rust along one side of its rear panels was poorly concealed behind a large hedge. All the windows were boarded up and it was partially hidden by the large willow trees that outlined the property. A Bank Owned sign hung lopsided by one hook in front of the tattered one-car garage, likely evidence that the recent owners had fallen victim to the current mortgage crisis and cleared out, leaving the house empty and available to vagrants or other unwanted lodgers. Like the one in it now.

"See anything?" Dan asked.

"Teigs's van, but there's no sign of movement."

"What's the plan?"

"I want you," she said pointing to Dan, "to go around to the west side of the house. Simons can cover the east side. I'm going around back. See if anything is out of place. No radios. No phones. Hand signals only. And don't go in alone. Copy?"

"Roger that," Dan said.

The three of them moved into position. Simons crouched behind a row of shrubs and signaled to Lee that the main house was empty and Tory's Porsche was in the garage. Even though Lee's arm and side protested, she bit back the pain and army-crawled through the mud, coming within a few feet of the battered shed behind the house. She ducked behind a tree and scanned for any movement out of the ordinary. A shadow suddenly appeared behind one of the covered windows and she placed her ear against it, straining to hear the conversation inside. She pulled her 9mm from its holster.

"Leave her alone," Tory yelled.

"I told you if I removed this gag you had to be quiet! You don't listen. Women must know their place. Now shut the fuck up!"

Lee found a small break in the structure and peered through it. She watched as Teigs grabbed a handful of Tory's hair and kissed her roughly.

"There," Teigs said. "That should satisfy you until I return." He pushed her back down to the floor and reapplied the gag. Picking Jo up awkwardly by the arms, he dragged her limp body outside to Tory's muffled protests.

"Oh, don't worry, my love," Teigs said. "She'll be awake for the finale. Don't go anywhere. I'll be back soon and we'll get our relationship started."

Lee watched, aching to move, but she waited until Teigs had Jo halfway out the door before she jumped him, knocking him to the ground and separating him from Jo, who still hadn't moved. He quickly scrambled to his feet and pulled out of his pocket a small rectangular device for Lee to see.

"You're dead, Teigs," she said, pointing her gun at his head. "Drop it."

Teigs laughed. "I knew you'd come."

"Didn't think you'd be surprised."

"Oh, I wasn't. You were always predictable, Winters. No one was as thorough as you. I remember well."

"If you remember, then you better put that down before I cut you in half."

"Your threats are useless. Put the gun away," he said, pointing to Jo, "or I'll blow her to kingdom come."

Lee holstered her weapon, her body between Jo and Teigs, which wasn't going to do much good if he decided to press that button. "It's down. Now tell me what you want."

"You, of course," he said as if she should know the answer. "I want you dead. I'm tired of hearing your name. When we served it was always *Winters did this, Winters said that.* I was so sick of hearing your name after the first year I promised to blow up the next guy that mentioned it." He chuckled evilly. "And when he did, I kept my promise."

"What the fuck are you talking about?" she said, narrowing her eyes.

"Remember Harrison?"

Harrison. Yes. She remembered him well. Trevor Harrison had been twenty-six years old and had less than a month to serve before his deployment in Iraq ended. His wife had recently given birth to a baby girl, and all he talked about the week before he died was how he couldn't wait to meet his new daughter. The day he died, he'd been working in the motor pool on a broken-down jeep when the engine suddenly exploded in his face. The debris nearly removed his head. He died instantly. The army had listed his death as an accident.

"Is it coming back?"

"You killed him? Why? He had a family—a daughter, for Christ's sake!"

"He was weak. All he talked about was how he wished he could be like you. He wanted a command, but instead the only thing he was able to do was put air in a tire. I did his bitch and that little brat a favor. Just like I'm going to do to Gary's and..." He paused, looking down at Jo's unmoving body. "What is she to you anyway? Have you fucked her yet?"

Lee pulled her gun in one fluid motion. She didn't want to ask the next question but she needed to know the answer. "The bomb...inside the building that day in Ramadi. Was that you too?"

"Yes." He laughed wildly and clapped his metallic hands like some kind of evil child. "You remember."

"Why? Why the fuck would you kill our men?"

"No." He pointed the remote at her. "I killed *your* men. Do you think I didn't know how they talked about me? How I was the butt of their jokes? I got trapped that day too, you know. I'd been ordered to set traps a few blocks away to keep out the insurgents but saw my opportunity to get rid of you so I took it. You kicked the door in and it fell on me as I was preparing the next bomb. I barely managed to get outside when the bomb blew. I lost my arms in that explosion, but at least I got rid of all of them. I took away what you cared about the most. That asshole Gary talked nonstop about his precious girlfriend and showed us all her picture all the damn time. He didn't deserve her. Now Tory will be mine, and this time I'll make sure there aren't enough pieces of you and your little bitch for the coroner to put together. I get everything I've ever wanted and you can go to hell."

Fury swept through Lee like a tidal wave. She hadn't been a casualty of war. She was purposely targeted—she and her men blown to pieces by one of their own. She'd lost her career, her friends, and her job, and she refused to allow this man to take anything else from her. Suddenly, the soldier she had been in Iraq returned with a vengeance. Her hands stopped trembling. Her eyes became eagle sharp. Her breathing was steady and barely discernible. Teigs must have sensed the change, because he suddenly looked a bit less confident.

"Move and I'll kill everyone!"

"Not if I kill you first."

Teigs pointed the remote in Lee's direction. Simons jumped out from behind one of the bushes and managed to knock it from his hand. Lee covered Jo's body protectively with her own, shielding her from the chaos going on around them. Simons lifted Teigs off the ground by one hand and threw him into a nearby tree, where he hit with a thud. Teigs surprised Simons and pulled a knife from his pocket, thrusting it into the larger man's calf. Simons howled in pain and Teigs lunged for the remote just as the sound of a gunshot split the air.

Teigs looked stunned as he crumpled to the ground, the detonator falling from his hand. Covered in a splatter of blood and tissue, he appeared lifeless, one solitary hole directly between his eyes.

"Thanks, Sarge," Simons grunted, letting out a shaky breath, his hands pressed to the knife wound.

"You're welcome and we're even," she said, suddenly remembering where she'd first met Corporal Ted Simons. He'd been the one to pull her from the building that day in Ramadi.

SECRETS AND SHADOWS

Simons had saved her life. But in and out of consciousness, she'd
never actually spoken to him. And he'd respected her enough as
a fellow soldier not to mention it when she'd met him at the West
home. He nodded at her in acknowledgement.

"What the hell happened here, Winters?" Agent Steele came
skidding around the corner and stared at Teigs's body.

"Agent Steele, glad you finally decided to join the party.
And I kept a promise," Lee said as she dropped to her knees and
examined Jo's injuries. She brushed a dirty strand of hair away
from her eyes. Jo groaned and Lee had never been so glad to see
someone come around.

"You came," Jo said weakly, touching Lee's forearm.

"Of course I did," Lee said, trying to contain her raging
emotions. She wanted to kiss Jo but didn't think it wise with the
new bruises on her face. Besides, everyone was watching.

"Oh, my God! That crazy guy with the weird eyes. Is he dead?"

"Yes," Lee whispered, "but don't look." She didn't realize
how much she'd missed Jo until she had her close enough to touch.
She shielded her from the commotion going on all around her,
trying to protect her emotionally as well as physically.

"Lee. What about Tory!?"

"Safe inside. But we need to get you checked out. Steele," she
said looking over her shoulder, "where the hell are the paramedics?"

"Two minutes out."

"See, you have to wait."

"Lee, please. I can tell my ribs are probably broken again, I
have a killer headache, and my face hurts like hell. But please. I
need to see her. To know she's okay."

"All right," she said, placing one arm under Jo for support. She
couldn't deny her anything, even though it was against her better
judgment. "Hold on to me and let me do all the work. Ready?"
She hoisted Jo to her feet, steadying her until she got her bearings.
They were about to walk toward the shed when Tory emerged,
sobbing into Gary's shoulder.

"Tory!"

"Jo?" she wiped her eyes. "Jo!" Tory ran to her and flung her arms around Jo's shoulders. Lee remained close, looming over the sisters like a guardian angel.

"Are you okay?" Tory asked.

"I would be if I could breathe," Jo said as Tory released her.

"Oh. Sorry, Sis. Are you sure? I was so scared. When he dragged you from the room…"

"Yeah, never better," Jo said, kissing Tory's forehead while keeping her eyes locked on Lee.

"Is that fucking freak show dead?"

"You betcha. Thanks to my bodyguard." Jo smiled up at Lee, who smiled back.

"Once again, you've proved beyond a doubt that you're invaluable, Lee," Tory said as Lee blushed. "Now can we get outta here? This place gives me the creeps."

Tory began to move away as Jo and Lee stood strong, a foot apart from one another, studying each other uncertainly. Tory excused herself, mumbling something about rejoining Gary.

"I wasn't sure if you'd find us in time," Jo finally said, looking as if she wanted to run her hands down Lee's body and make sure there were no holes in it.

"With you in danger, how could I not?" Lee's voice was raw with emotion. She'd almost lost her, the one person that made life worth living. As she stood looking at Jo, she didn't want to hide behind any more barriers. She wanted to tear them all down, to try to be the person Jo thought her to be. She wanted everything Jo had to give, and she wanted to prove that she would never take the chance of losing her again. "We should go."

"Yes, we should, but not before you make me a promise."

"What promise?"

"Promise me when we get back that you won't disappear again right away. That you'll give us a chance to talk. Please."

Lee pulled Jo into the security of her arms. She didn't give a damn what other people would think. "I promise. I'm not going anywhere."

CHAPTER TWENTY-SIX

The next day Jo pulled into Lee's apartment complex and turned off the engine. She'd wanted to meet up earlier, but Lee had said it would take a while for the police to question her regarding the shooting, though she was almost positive no charges would be brought against her due to the circumstances. When Lee had called to say she was finished, Jo had hurriedly said good-bye to Tory, leaving her and Gary at the house to talk about where their relationship was headed, if anywhere at all.

Gary had cried when Jo had returned the wallet-sized picture of Tory that Lee had taken off Teigs's dead body. He thought he'd misplaced it while serving in Iraq and remembered showing it off to the guys one evening, but he wasn't sure how it fell into Teigs's possession. Gary told Jo in confidence that he didn't know what the future held for him and Tory, but for the first time in a long time he was starting to believe in the possibility of one.

She'd paid close attention to Gary and Tory's interactions and was beginning to understand that all soldiers really were alike. They'd sacrifice everything to protect the ones they loved, even if that meant keeping themselves apart. She'd wasted too much time thinking about herself during this whole ordeal and not enough time considering how Lee had spent her life before she became a part of it.

She finally understood what kept Lee's walls up, what kept all soldiers from sharing their pain. They had to prove they were strong. But more important, they had to protect the ones they loved even if they had to suffer to do it. She wanted Lee to know that she would never have to suffer alone any more. She would be there for her always and forever, if she let her.

"Lee, open up," Jo said as she knocked on the wooden door separating her from all she loved. The longer the door went unanswered, the more Jo feared that maybe Lee had changed her mind. *Maybe she's not home. Maybe she left me again. Maybe—*

"Hey." Lee yanked open the door and, for the first time, her smile was open and unguarded.

Jo didn't wait for an invitation. Instead she pushed her way into Lee's apartment and waited in anticipation for Lee to close the door. The second the lock clicked into place, she threw her arms around Lee's neck and pulled her down for a kiss, throwing all her passion into that one heated meeting of lips. Her ribs protested and her face hurt, but she didn't care. Lee was the balm for her aching mind, body, and soul.

"Wait." Lee gasped.

"I'm tired of waiting. Tell me you don't want me or this?"

"I can't."

"Can't what?"

Lee lifted Jo's chin so she could press her lips to Jo's. "Can't tell you no."

The kiss started out slow. It was a kiss that spoke of understanding and a knowledge of being with the person who challenged your mind and connected with your heart. It spoke of promises yet to come and days filled with new memories. When they broke for air, the shadows faded and the world was brighter than it had been in a long time.

"We should talk," Lee said before her legs nearly buckled from Jo's firm but insistent strokes against her chest. It felt like Jo's hands were everywhere at once, and Lee's whole body was on fire with desire.

"Yes, we should and I promise we will. But this second, the only thing on my mind is to be naked and in your arms. What do you say, soldier?"

Lee answered with a groan and walked Jo backward toward her bedroom, kissing her lips, cheeks, neck. Jo pulled Lee's shirttail from her trousers, and her abdomen tightened under the tingle of Jo's nails raking over the skin.

"Your body is a work of art."

"Hardly. You're the beautiful one." Lee gently laid Jo onto the bed and helped her strip out of her clothes, mindful of her injuries. She then stripped quickly before lying astride Jo, throwing a muscled thigh over her non-injured leg. "I don't want to hurt you."

"Don't worry, darling. You won't."

Lee propped herself up on her good arm and trailed kisses down the side of Jo's neck with her tongue and teeth. "God, you taste and smell incredible. I've dreamt of this moment every night."

Taking her time, Lee covered every square inch of Jo with soft kisses and firm strokes of her hands. Jo hissed as Lee sucked on one of her nipples, releasing it with a pop.

"Bite me," Jo said, pushing her nipple farther into Lee's mouth. Jo reached for one of Lee's hands and placed it between her legs.

Lee slid two of her fingers up and down Jo's clitoris, exalting in the wetness against her palm. She gently tugged and Jo gasped, but refused to enter until she begged.

"Oh no, you don't." Jo grasped Lee's hand and thrust two fingers inside her. "You can tease me all you want another time. I've waited for you long enough. Yeah, that's right, baby. Make me yours."

Lee buried her face in the crook of Jo's neck and thrust deeply into her. Jo's body greedily engulfed Lee's hand, but Lee still held back, afraid of her strength, afraid of hurting Jo when her own need was so great.

"Deeper," Jo moaned, her hips meeting every one of Lee's thrusts.

"I want to. Believe me. But I'm scared of my hunger for you."

Jo looked deeply into Lee's eyes, the pure look of desire and lust nearly sending Lee over the edge. "When will you understand, you're all I need. You can't hurt me. Loving me can't hurt me, sweetheart."

Lee flipped onto her back, positioning Jo above her to straddle her hips. She kept her hand buried deep inside her and grasped her hips with her free hand to hold her in place. Jo leaned forward and Lee took a rose-tipped nipple between her teeth. She matched every bite on the firm tip with a matching stroke over Jo's clitoris, and every pull was in time with the thrust of Jo's hips that buried her hand deeper and deeper until she felt Jo's passion crest. "Let it go. Come for me, baby."

"I can't stop. I…oh."

Jo rode Lee's hand frantically and the muscles around it began to tighten and tremble. Moisture dripped down Lee's arm and onto her belly as she pushed farther still. But it wasn't enough. Thrusting into Jo and holding nothing back, she held on tight as Jo's muscles spasmed, enveloping her fingers in the warm, tight cocoon of Jo's ecstasy.

Jo pitched forward and braced both arms above Lee's head. She thrust hard onto Lee's hand, crying out as Lee strummed her thumb rhythmically over her clitoris. "Yes, right there. Oh…don't stop."

"Never."

Lee nibbled on a pebbled nipple as Jo's entire body tensed on the brink of exploding again. Screaming out Lee's name, Jo rode out wave after wave of pure pleasure, but it still wasn't enough as a stronger, more powerful surge built deep inside. Sensing Jo's need, Lee stood up and cradled Jo with her good arm, pinning her against the bedroom wall. With the added support of the wall behind them, Lee surged against Jo, brushing her own clit as well with every thrust of her pistoning hips.

"That's it, baby." Jo panted. "It's yours. Take it."

They cried out as they orgasmed together, riding the waves of ecstasy hard and fast. Since her legs were shaking, Lee decided they'd better lie down again. With Jo's legs wrapped around her hips she moved them back to the bed and lay beside Jo, pulling her tightly to her side.

"Beautiful," Lee whispered, holding Jo's trembling body.

"Wow," Jo said. "That was incredible."

"Yeah, it was. You okay?"

"Never better," Jo said, tracing the outline of Lee's sculpted abs. Lee groaned, the touch unleashing the desire she had kept trapped inside for a long time. "But you're not. Seems someone needs attention."

Lee gasped when Jo's fingers entered her without warning. She felt Jo slide between her legs. "Oh, God," Lee said, grasping the sheets. "I want you so bad it hurts."

"Not for long." Jo moved her tongue along Lee's clitoris as Lee rewarded her with a groan. "Like that, do ya?"

"Yes."

"Is this for me?" Jo pulled back the hood, toying with Lee, who squirmed above her. "You didn't answer my question."

Lee tried to focus but every nerve ending in her body had suddenly come alive. Jo licked her slowly, teasing around her clit up and down in no particular rhythm but refusing to touch her where she needed it the most. She wanted to answer but lost the words on a strangled plea.

"Tell me what I want to hear, sweetheart." Jo used the tip of her tongue to toy with Lee's clit once more.

"Please, baby. Do that…a little harder."

"Tell me what I want to hear or I'll make you suffer."

"Harder…press harder."

"Not until you tell me what I want to hear."

"Christ, can't think. Need you to…suck me."

"I will. I promise." Jo licked her again. "Now once more, is this for me?"

"Yes, it's for you. Only for you. Always for you."

The second Jo took mercy on Lee and took her into her mouth, Lee's back arched and she came with a shout. Jo held on, only releasing her hold when Lee quieted and sagged against the sheets. When Jo moved to recline in her arms, Lee pulled her close and closed her eyes, thinking that, for the first time in her life, she'd finally found the place she belonged. She had found home.

❖

It could have been minutes or even hours later when Lee awoke with Jo cradled in her arms. Glancing down the length of their bodies, she enjoyed the view of their intertwined limbs. She had no idea where their relationship would go from here. All she knew was that there was no way they could go back to the way things were.

"What are you thinking about?" Lee asked, as she twirled a few strands of Jo's golden hair between her fingers.

"That I shouldn't have allowed you to push me away."

"I'm sorry."

Jo moved so she could look at Lee's face. She placed a palm on the center of her chest, holding her in place. "Not good enough."

"Jo—"

"Hush…I'm not finished. I was also thinking about how you must be feeling about all of this. I'm sorry I never asked you."

"Don't ever apologize to me for what's between us. If you want to ask me something, just ask."

There it was. The door had been fully opened, offering Jo permanent entrance. "Tell me what scares you."

Lee's breath caught in her throat. What did she ever do to deserve someone like Jo? Words failed her, and to her horror, the tears she should have shed years ago started to fall.

"Oh, sweetheart, it's okay. I'm here. I'll always be here for you." Jo repeated the beautiful statement over and over, holding Lee to her chest. "I know you're in pain. I can see it in your eyes. But know I'm willing to stand by your side and make the commitment to love you no matter what."

"I'm sorry," Lee said, wiping at her tear-stained cheeks. "That's never happened before."

"You mean to tell me you've never cried?"

"No. Never," Lee said, more controlled, almost angry. "I'm a soldier. We don't cry." Christ, could the situation get any more embarrassing? Shaking. Crying. Talk about a goddamned disgrace.

"Jesus, Lee. I don't know what kind of crap they feed you in the military, but damn it, you're human. Flesh and blood. You're the woman I love." Jo knelt on the bed and pulled Lee close. "Let me in, baby. Don't hide from me. I saw firsthand what the war did to Gary and Tory's relationship. I promise it won't come between us, no matter what the price."

"Jo," Lee said in a pained whisper. "You don't know what you're asking."

"Then tell me, darling. Explain to me what hurts you. I want to help. I do. But you have to give me that chance."

"Don't you think I want to? Can't you see there are things about me that you're not aware of yet? Things I'm not particularly proud of. You may want to leave as soon as you find out, and I wouldn't blame you."

Jo pushed Lee back onto the bed and straddled her hips. She grabbed Lee's hands and pinned them above her head. "Damn it, Lee. Look at me. What do you see in my eyes?"

Lee inhaled deeply, staring into the sea of blue. "My whole world."

Tears rolled down Jo's cheeks unchecked and she smiled. "I love you so much. Please, Lee. Tell me."

"I'm going to tell you a story," she said struggling with her own emotions. "There'd been a time when hopelessness consumed my life. I had nearly lost my arm, my troops, and my command. I was thrust into a swirling void of despair. I'd felt useless, out of control. Encouraging words from other soldiers and therapists were futile, and I sank into a deep depression. Some, like Gary, even thought I'd snap from the pressure. The day my discharge papers arrived, I'd never felt so inadequate or lost. They told me I'd never be fit for duty, wouldn't be able to support a rifle, couldn't lift a man on my shoulders or carry out the numerous duties I'd performed a hundred times. Without my command and my troops,

I had nothing left. What you don't know is that I suffered more than just a physical injury during the war."

"PTSD." It wasn't a question.

"Yeah. I can't control it and my symptoms are getting worse."

"I wrote a paper on PTSD in my college psych class. I recall my teacher telling me that the symptoms were as serious and debilitating as any physical injury. Will you tell me your symptoms?"

Lee focused on some irrelevant spot on the wall. "They weren't too bad at first. My hands shake. Then there's the sweating, the racing heart, and sometimes I forget what I'm going to say. I forget details, and in my current line of work that could be dangerous for the person I'm trying to protect."

Lee expected a lot of reactions from Jo, but outright laughter wasn't one of them. What the hell could she possibly find so amusing?

"And you say it's been getting worse?" Jo asked, a little more serious now.

"Yes."

"Since when?"

"Since we met."

Jo let go of Lee's hands and stretched her body out on top of Lee's. She threw her arms around Lee's neck and kissed her soundly. "Do you want to hear something funny?"

"Not particularly," Lee said, still trying to figure out Jo's strange reaction to her life-altering declaration.

"I suffer those same symptoms too."

"Jo," Lee growled. "This isn't a game. I could hurt you…in my sleep. I do things sometimes when I'm not aware. You may not be safe with me, love. There are nightmares. Sometimes it's like I'm back in that God-forsaken desert and I panic. I couldn't live with myself if I hurt you."

"You listen to me, Lee Winters." Jo slid her body up and down, rubbing her wet center against Lee's soft skin. "I am safer with you than with anyone else in my life. You've never hurt me…

not once, do you hear?" Jo said softly but fiercely. "I understand that PTSD is serious and I swear I'll help you get through whatever we need to do to help you get better. But you see, since we met, I've been experiencing those symptoms too. I can't sleep. I have trouble eating sometimes. My hands sweat when you're near. My heart races when you touch me, and I can't think when you say my name the way only you can. Do you know why?"

Lee couldn't speak, too wrapped up in the way Jo's lips moved to think.

"It's because I'm in love with you."

The dam inside Lee's heart burst and all her emotions rushed out at once. Jo had set her free, and there was nothing she wanted more in her life than to prove to Jo just how much that meant. "I love you. I do. With everything in me," Lee said, rolling Jo over to cover Jo's body with her own.

"'Bout damn time, soldier. Now, I command you to kiss me."

"Yes, ma'am."

About the Author

L.T. Marie spends most of her time working out and writes during her free time. Her hobbies are reading every lesbian romance she can get her hands on and watching Giants baseball. She is the author of *Three Days* and *One Touch*.

Books Available from Bold Strokes Books

Date with Destiny by Mason Dixon. When sophisticated bank executive Rashida Ivey meets unemployed blue collar worker Destiny Jackson, will her life ever be the same? (978-1-60282-878-0)

The Devil's Orchard by Ali Vali. Cain and Emma plan a wedding before the birth of their third child while Juan Luis is still lurking, and as Cain plans for his death, an unexpected visitor arrives and challenges her belief in her father, Dalton Casey. (978-1-60282-879-7)

Secrets and Shadows by L.T. Marie. A bodyguard and the woman she protects run from a madman and into each other's arms. (978-1-60282-880-3)

Change Horizon: Three Novellas by Gun Brooke. Three stories of courageous women who dare to love as they fight to claim a future in a hostile universe. (978-1-60282-881-0)

Scarlett Thirst by Crin Claxton. When hot, feisty Rani meets cool, vampire Rob, one lifetime isn't enough, and the road from human to vampire is shorter than you think… (978-1-60282-856-8)

Battle Axe by Carsen Taite. How close is too close? Bounty hunter Luca Bennett will soon find out. (978-1-60282-871-1)

Improvisation by Karis Walsh. High school geometry teacher Jan Carroll thinks she's figured out the shape of her life and her future, until graphic artist and fiddle player Tina Nelson comes along and teaches her to improvise. (978-1-60282-872-8)

For Want of a Fiend by Barbara Ann Wright. Without her Fiendish power, can Princess Katya and her consort Starbride stop a magic-wielding madman from sparking an uprising in the kingdom of Farraday? (978-1-60282-873-5)

Broken in Soft Places by Fiona Zedde. The instant Sara Chambers meets the seductive and sinful Merille Thompson, she falls hard, but knowing the difference between love and a dangerous, all-consuming desire is just one of the lessons Sara must learn before it's too late. (978-1-60282-876-6)

Healing Hearts by Donna K. Ford. Running from tragedy, the women of Willow Springs find that with friendship, there is hope, and with love, there is everything. (978-1-60282-877-3)

Desolation Point by Cari Hunter. When a storm strands Sarah Kent in the North Cascades, Alex Pascal is determined to find her. Neither imagines the dangers they will face when a ruthless criminal begins to hunt them down. (978-1-60282-865-0)

I Remember by Julie Cannon. What happens when you can never forget the first kiss, the first touch, the first taste of lips on skin? What happens when you know you will remember every single detail of a mysterious woman? (978-1-60282-866-7)

The Gemini Deception by Kim Baldwin and Xenia Alexiou. The truth, the whole truth, and nothing but lies. Book six in the Elite Operatives series. (978-1-60282-867-4)

Scarlet Revenge by Sheri Lewis Wohl. When faith alone isn't enough, will the love of one woman be strong enough to save a vampire from damnation? (978-1-60282-868-1)

Ghost Trio by Lillian Q. Irwin. When Lee Howe hears the voice of her dead lover singing to her, is it a hallucination, a ghost, or something more sinister? (978-1-60282-869-8)

The Princess Affair by Nell Stark. Rhodes Scholar Kerry Donovan arrives at Oxford ready to focus on her studies, but her life and her priorities are thrown into chaos when she catches the eye of Her Royal Highness Princess Sasha. (978-1-60282-858-2)

The Chase by Jesse J. Thoma. When Isabelle Rochat's life is threatened, she receives the unwelcome protection and attention of bounty hunter Holt Lasher who vows to keep Isabelle safe at all costs. (978-1-60282-859-9)

The Lone Hunt by L.L. Raand. In a world where humans and praeterns conspire for the ultimate power, violence is a way of life…and death. A Midnight Hunters novel. (978-1-60282-860-5)

The Supernatural Detective by Crin Claxton. Tony Carson sees dead people. With a drag queen for a spirit guide and a devastatingly attractive herbalist for a client, she's about to discover the spirit world can be a very dangerous world indeed. (978-1-60282-861-2)

Beloved Gomorrah by Justine Saracen. Undersea artists creating their own City on the Plain uncover the truth about Sodom and Gomorrah, whose "one righteous man" is a murderer, rapist, and conspirator in genocide. (978-1-60282-862-9)

Cut to the Chase by Lisa Girolami. Careful and methodical author Paige Cornish falls for brash and wild Hollywood actress Avalon Randolph, but can these opposites find a happy middle ground in a town that never lives in the middle? (978-1-60282-783-7)

More Than Friends by Erin Dutton. Evelyn Fisher thinks she has the perfect role model for a long-term relationship, until her best friends, Kendall and Melanie, split up and all three women must reevaluate their lives and their relationships. (978-1-60282-784-4)

Every Second Counts by D. Jackson Leigh. Every second counts in Bridgette LeRoy's desperate mission to protect her heart and stop Marc Ryder's suicidal return to riding rodeo bulls. (978-1-60282-785-1)

Dirty Money by Ashley Bartlett. Vivian Cooper and Reese DiGiovanni just found out that falling in love is hard. It's even harder when you're running for your life. (978-1-60282-786-8)

Sea Glass Inn by Karis Walsh. When Melinda Andrews commissions a series of mosaics by Pamela Whitford for her new inn, she doesn't expect to be more captivated by the artist than by the paintings. (978-1-60282-771-4)

The Awakening: A Sisters of Spirits novel by Yvonne Heidt. Sunny Skye has interacted with spirits her entire life, but when she runs into Officer Jordan Lawson during a ghost investigation, she discovers more than just facts in a missing girl's cold case file. (978-1-60282-772-1)

Murphy's Law by Yolanda Wallace. No matter how high you climb, you can't escape your past. (978-1-60282-773-8)

Blacker Than Blue by Rebekah Weatherspoon. Threatened with losing her first love to a powerful demon, vampire Cleo Jones is willing to break the ultimate law of the undead to rebuild the family she has lost. (978-1-60282-774-5)

Silver Collar by Gill McKnight. Werewolf Luc Garoul is outlawed and out of control, but can her family track her down before a sinister predator gets there first? Fourth in the Garoul series. (978-1-60282-764-6)

The Dragon Tree Legacy by Ali Vali. For Aubrey Tarver time hasn't dulled the pain of losing her first love Wiley Gremillion, but she has to set that aside when her choices put her life and her family's lives in real danger. (978-1-60282-765-3)

The Midnight Room by Ronica Black. After a chance encounter with the mysterious and brooding Lillian Gray in the "midnight room" of The Griffin, a local lesbian bar, confident and gorgeous Audrey McCarthy learns that her bad-girl behavior isn't bulletproof. (978-1-60282-766-0)

Dirty Sex by Ashley Bartlett. Vivian Cooper and twins Reese and Ryan DiGiovanni stole a lot of money and the guy they took it from wants it back. Like now. (978-1-60282-767-7)

The Storm by Shelley Thrasher. Rural East Texas. 1918. War-weary Jaq Bergeron and marriage-scarred musician Molly Russell try to salvage love from the devastation of the war abroad and natural disasters at home. (978-1-60282-780-6)

Crossroads by Radclyffe. Dr. Hollis Monroe specializes in short-term relationships but when she meets pregnant mother-to-be Annie Colfax, fate brings them together at a crossroads that will change their lives forever. (978-1-60282-756-1)